SECOND CHANCE CHRISTMAS

ALEXA RIVERS

To Kayne
For your unwavering belief in me.

*E*vie Parata kicked the door of her new-to-her car and screamed in frustration.

Could this day get any worse?

A pair of little old ladies stared at her and tittered behind their hands, but Evie ignored them. She was used to the gossip of Itirangi, the tiny New Zealand town where she'd grown up, and was now stuck in, courtesy of her crappy ride.

"Filthy, slimeball salesman," she muttered to herself, stalking up the pavement and back again. When the guy had sold her the car this morning, taking the majority of her savings, he'd promised it was in good working order, and that had certainly seemed to be true. The battered Subaru had seen better days, but when she'd taken it for a test drive, she hadn't had any troubles. Not that Evie really knew anything about cars, since she'd spent the past nine years using public transportation.

Still, she'd been itching to have her own wheels for months now, and the timing had seemed opportune—she'd encountered the second-hand dealership on her walk to the bus stop in Dunedin where she'd planned to catch a ride to Timaru. On impulse, she'd purchased the Subaru instead.

Two birds, one stone, or so she'd thought. Now it seemed the car might not even last the rest of the three-hour drive.

Hopping behind the wheel, she turned the key in the ignition again. The engine flipped over once, then sputtered out, and she swore under her breath.

Don't panic.

There was a mechanic less than a block away. From here, she couldn't tell if it was open, so she locked the stupid car to protect her worldly goods, which were neatly packed into a suitcase in the back seat, then jogged toward the garage. Unfortunately, the signs had already been taken in, and the lights inside were turned off. She groaned, resting her hands on her thighs as she caught her breath. *Damn.*

Never one to take no for an answer, she bashed on the door. "Open up!"

No one came. She pounded harder. Still nothing. Ducking around the side of the building, she checked the other doors. All shut and locked. Everyone had cleared out for the day, and it was only four-thirty on Christmas Eve. Not even Christmas yet. She shouldn't be surprised. Itirangi had never been a thriving hub of activity.

She trekked back around to the front door and called the contact number painted on the glass. Inside, a phone rang. She crossed her fingers, hoping the landline would redirect to a cell, but no such luck. A recorded message asked her to leave her name and details and they would get back to her on Boxing Day.

She sank to the pavement, buried her face in her hands and growled. This is what she got for impulse-buying. She couldn't afford to be stranded in Itirangi. She needed to get to her friend Monica's orchard, where she had an invitation to pick berries while she figured out what the hell she was doing with her life.

She straightened, brushed off the uncertainty that threatened to crush her every time she dwelled on her future, and used her phone's internet browser to search for other mechanics in the area. The nearest open workshop was twenty miles away, and when she called to ask about a tow service, the friendly voice on the other end quoted a price that made her jaw drop.

She hung up and wiped her palms on her denim shorts. Despite the cloud overhead, it was a muggy, stifling day. Beads of sweat had broken out on her upper lip and at her temples. She drew in a calming breath. Getting her rage-face on wouldn't help anybody. She needed to be smart here. What were her options?

It should be simple. Her best friends in the world lived here. If she called one of them, she had no doubt they'd drop whatever they were doing to rescue her, but she was sick and tired of being rescued, and she didn't want to mess up her friends' holiday plans. They'd all settled down with partners this year and were probably spending Christmas Eve with their families, as they ought to. She didn't want to impose, especially not when she wasn't feeling her usual self.

For as long as she could remember, she'd been the wild one, the girl who was always ready to party, the one who never turned down a dare. But this would be her first Christmas alone. The first since her mother passed away right here in this sleepy little town. Grief gripped her, digging its icy claws into her heart, and her throat constricted. She blinked away tears.

If she called her friends and pretended everything was fine, they'd see right through her in an instant, and if she was honest with them about everything she was keeping bottled up inside, she'd be a blubbering wreck at the slightest hint of concern or empathy. No, she needed to be alone, so she could honor her mother's traditions and hole up with some donuts, a bottle of wine, and *The Little Match Girl* by Hans Christian Andersen.

Apart from calling her friends, what other options did she

have? The buses had finished until Boxing Day, and she didn't have the money for a taxi. With a heavy sigh, she resigned herself to staying in her car. She had blankets, and the back seat folded down. She'd get through the holiday just fine. It wasn't like she'd planned anything fancy, and the 24-hour convenience store would be open all day tomorrow so she could buy enough food to get her through. She'd weathered worse. Mind made up, she returned to the car, cursing the oppressive heat once again. What she wouldn't give for a shower.

She ducked inside the car and slipped her sunglasses on to mask her face, wishing she'd had the foresight to purchase her usual ten-dollar bottle of Moscato before she'd left Dunedin, rather than stopping by the liquor store here, which happened to be located next to Davy's Bar. Now she had wine, but no working transportation to escape in, and Davy O'Connor was the last person she wanted to see.

Since breaking his tender teenage heart, she'd habitually avoided him to the best of her ability. It was impossible to distance herself completely given they shared mutual friends, but she tried to train her focus elsewhere whenever they were forced into proximity. She told herself she kept away from him because of how painfully their relationship had ended, but if she were honest, what hurt most was the thought of what they could have had together if she'd cared to stick around.

She shrank lower in the seat. Hopefully Davy was out of town. Her pride couldn't stand for him to see her living in her car outside his bar. How he'd laugh to see her reduced to this after she'd brashly declared herself a woman of the world and breezed out of Itirangi, full of misplaced confidence.

Reclining the seat backward, she removed her glasses, curled onto her side and closed her eyes. If she napped the time away, it would pass faster, and she'd mastered the art of napping on cue. A few moments later, she dozed off.

She woke when a drop of water splashed onto her eyelid, and opened her eyes just in time for a second one to land.

"Ugh," she muttered, swiping it away as the drips began in earnest.

Someone knocked on the window, and she bolted upright, thumping her knee on the bottom of the steering wheel. Breath hissed between her teeth. She glanced up, and then the impossible happened. Her day got worse.

It wasn't enough for her to waste all her money on a broken car and get stranded with rain leaking through the roof. To top it off, Davy O'Connor had witnessed her humiliation. Just bloody fantastic.

He gestured for her to wind down the window. She deliberately took her time, delaying the inevitable while oddly fascinated by the way the downpour soaked through his clothes and trickled from the tips of his dark red hair.

"Hi, Evelyn," he said in his lilting Irish accent. "Car trouble?"

Evie winced. He was the only person who called her by her full name, and it made her feel seventeen again. "What's it to you?"

He shook his head, droplets of water scattering in every direction, some landing on her, then he smiled. The prick. "Can I call one of the girls to come get you?" he asked. "You'll be sitting out here all night, otherwise. Won't find anyone to fix your car this late."

"Don't call the girls," Evie said quickly. Too quickly.

His eyes narrowed. "Have you not told them you're around?"

She tried not to look guilty. She knew she wasn't being the best friend by avoiding them, but she needed privacy to lick her wounds. "I'm only passing through. Didn't seem like there was any point."

"Bullshite. You know Aria would love to have you over for Christmas." His gaze became sympathetic. "Especially this year."

This year. She knew exactly what he meant, and her throat clogged with emotion. *He'd remembered.* She'd seen him at the funeral, and vaguely recalled being wrapped in his arms, but the hug had been over too soon, and she'd been out of her mind with grief. They may not have even spoken because he'd been just one in a long line of people wanting to offer their condolences.

"I'm sorry about your mum," he said, as though reading her mind. "The holiday season must be hard for you."

It was—more so than she'd expected—but she wasn't one to show weakness, especially not to him. "I'm getting by."

His brow crinkled, and rain dripped from his nose. "You should be with your friends."

"I can't," she whispered, hating to admit it. Her skin crawled at the prospect of being forced to smile and keep her emotions hidden so she wouldn't ruin the day for anyone else. "Aria has Eli and the baby. Sophie has Cooper. Avery has Gareth. I love those girls like crazy, but I can't be around all that cheerfulness right now." Not when all she wanted to do was hug her photo of her mum to her chest, and cry.

Davy softened. "Why don't you come upstairs then? You can dry off and we'll talk about what to do next. You can't stay in this crappy old car, and I've got plenty of space."

Evie bristled at the insult to her vehicle, even if she privately agreed, and at the implication that she needed him to fix her problems. She wasn't about to melt into a helpless puddle of femininity just because her ex had caught her at a fragile moment. Despite everything, she had her pride. "Just watch me."

With that, she wound up the window, shifted her body to avoid the stream of water coming through the roof, and ignored him. She could wait this weather out. It was a sun shower. How long could it last?

～

Stubborn fool woman.

Davy watched Evelyn through the window of his second-story apartment. She had too much pride for her own good, shivering in her car just to prove she didn't need him, as if he didn't already know. He moved away from the window and strung another strand of star-shaped lights, listening to the drum of rain outside and trying to ignore the tug of his conscience. He'd done the right thing. It wasn't his fault if she drowned out there.

He turned up the volume of the Christmas carols playing through a Bluetooth speaker and started arranging red baubles on the tree in the corner of his lounge. It had been cut only yesterday, and the scent of pine sap wafted through the air. He enjoyed decorating, even if it was only intended to take his mind off the other job he desperately needed to do.

His thoughts drifted back to Evelyn. She was also a distraction, albeit an unwelcome one. The woman was a gorgeous livewire but seeing her made him feel like an awkward teenager again, bringing back all the intense emotions he hadn't experienced since he'd been with her. She appealed to him like no one else, and for all he'd tried to rid himself of his attraction to her, he'd had no luck.

When he'd glimpsed her out the window earlier, bent over the hood of her car, he hadn't been able to resist checking her out. He'd chuckled as she booted the car and stomped away, then when she'd returned, he'd waited for her to leave. Except she hadn't. It seemed Evelyn was stuck. In Itirangi. Outside his bar. And determined to suffer rather than let him help her when she was sad and vulnerable.

7

The Almighty had a sick sense of humor.

Finishing with the baubles, he wandered across the hall to the kitchen, which was separated from his dining area by two long counters. It was the first room he'd remodeled after buying the place, knocking out a wall to make a welcoming open plan area. He checked the timer and flicked the oven light on. The sponge cakes he'd put in to bake earlier had risen nicely and were golden brown on top. He inched the door open and inserted a skewer into each, to check whether the batter was cooked through. *Perfect.*

Donning oven mitts, he pulled the door all the way down, retrieved the cakes, and carried them to the counter to cool. He inhaled the delicious scent. Mm. There was nothing he loved more than the smell of freshly baked cake.

The rain outside thundered even louder. Wincing, he returned to the living room window and peered out. Evelyn hadn't left her car. He'd seen how badly the roof leaked. She'd be drenched by now.

Not my problem.

Turning away, he collected a pack of candy canes from the coffee table and hung them on the tree. He was whistling along to Snoopy's Christmas and scrubbing cake tins when a high-pitched beep sounded above the music. The doorbell. He opened the window and leaned out. The beep sounded again.

He grinned down at the bedraggled woman on his doorstep. "Oh, Miss Evelyn. How times have changed."

She hadn't heard him. Her shoulders hunched, and she jabbed the doorbell repeatedly.

"Can I help you?" he called, laughing when her head snapped up and she glared at him.

"Don't just stand there," she yelled. "Let me in!"

"Are you sure you want to come in?" he asked. "That car looks mighty comfortable."

Her hands went to her hips. "Please, Davy," she said, syrupy sweet. "May I come in and dry off?"

He closed the window, amused when her mouth dropped open, but against his better judgement, he hurried downstairs to let her in just as she was storming back to her car, cursing creatively.

"Come in, silly girl."

She spun around, and up close he could see the water dripping from the ends of her shoulder-length dark hair onto her shoulders and then under the rounded neckline of her shirt. One trail of water dipped into the valley between her breasts, which were partially exposed. He tore his attention from her chest before she noticed. Been there, done that. Had the emotional scars to prove it.

Evelyn scowled at him, every bit a bad-tempered Fae Queen seeking to bring mortal men to their knees. She fetched her suitcase from the back seat and swept past him up the stairs, coming to a stop outside his apartment door. "You going to open it for me, or what?"

2

For a moment, Evie thought he might refuse. He stared up at her, as if unsure how she'd arrived, wet as a freaking drowned rat, inside his bar. If he kicked her out, that would be the icing on her humiliation cake. She was cold and miserable, marooned with hardly any money, alone for Christmas, and now the person most likely to rub it all in her face was witnessing her low point.

Lifting her chin, she eyed him expectantly. She'd never let on how much it cost her to ring his doorbell. Not even if she lived to be a hundred years old. "Well?"

He strode up the stairs to her side, making the stairwell oddly claustrophobic, shoved the door open, and waved her in. "Go right ahead. Make yourself at home."

She could hear the irony in his voice, but frankly, she was so relieved to be out of the rain she didn't care. The door opened onto a long hallway. If she remembered correctly, the upstairs area had been a hotel before Davy purchased the bar, and it had retained that layout, with a number of rooms coming off a central corridor.

"Fourth room on the right is the spare bedroom," he told her. "Drop your suitcase in there and have a shower. There's a towel on the bed. The bathroom is directly opposite. I assume you have some dry clothes."

"As long as the water didn't get into my suitcase." Which it could well have done, while she was busy with her head stuck up her ass. When would she learn that biting off her nose to spite her face got her nowhere? Her pride be damned. It was more important to be warm and dry.

"And whose fault would it be if it did?" he demanded.

"Yeah, yeah." Rolling her eyes, she left him standing in the hallway, went to the room he'd indicated and laid her case on the floor. A double bed occupied the center of the space, with a standing wardrobe at its foot and a small cabinet beside the pillow. Other than that, the room was empty.

She unzipped her suitcase and touched the top layer of clothing. Slightly damp but not bad, all things considered. She hung the damp items on hangers in the wardrobe, gathered her toiletries, and crossed the hallway to the bathroom, which was a repurposed guest room, easily as large as the room she'd come from. A bathtub took up half of one wall, large enough for Davy's rangy frame, and the floor and walls were tiled, with a shower head in the corner opposite the bath.

She vacillated between the bath and the shower, but when an image of Davy lying naked beneath a layer of bubbles flashed through her mind, she opted for the shower. The last thing she needed was to get hot and flustered over a man she'd loved and left.

As quick as humanly possible, she peeled off her soggy clothes and got under a scalding hot jet of water, sighing happily as her skin prickled and started to warm. She soaped, shampooed, rinsed, and just stood beneath the spray for several minutes. By the time she shut the water off, she felt a thousand percent better than she had going in. She dried herself, wrapped a towel around her hair and another around her body, then wrung out her wet clothing and tucked them beneath her arm. When she opened the door, steam billowed out into the hall. She stepped onto fluffy carpet, luxuriating in the softness of it against her bare feet, and looked up.

Then she froze. So did Davy, who'd emerged from the spare bedroom, where she'd left her things.

"Erm," he said, then swallowed, the cords of his throat working. His eyes widened as they traveled from her bare shoulders to her concealed breasts and down her exposed legs. She pulled the towel tighter around her chest. She wasn't what one would call shy about her body, but she felt vulnerable enough without being actually naked in front of him.

"Yes?" she asked, raising an eyebrow.

"I, erm." His eyes darted back to her face, his cheeks taking on a sunburned hue. "I left a clotheshorse in your room, in case you need it."

"Thanks." She waited for him to move, since he was standing between her and her belongings, but his feet seemed to be fastened to the floor. "Do you mind?"

"Oh, sorry." He shuffled away, head down, the blush spreading down the back of his neck. Despite her best intentions, Evie found his embarrassment endearing. It wasn't often that a capable, talkative man like him was at a loss for words, and she was flattered that he found her attractive. Part of her wondered if he'd still react that way to her body if she'd stayed with him after high school, as he'd wanted, or would the novelty have worn off?

No, don't go down that road.

Hurrying into the bedroom, she closed the door with a soft click and leaned against it. *You made your decision,* she reminded herself. *You don't get to have second thoughts now.*

Evie could admit her weaknesses. She was flighty, scattered and temperamental, but she'd always been smart. Too smart to be dwelling on "what ifs" and the mossy green of Davy O'Connor's eyes. She dressed, then withdrew a small fleece blanket from the bottom of her suitcase. From within the folded blanket she extracted a photo frame, then wiped the glass and placed it on the bedside cabinet. She studied the photograph, which showed a petite Maori woman with straight bangs and a short ponytail, her arm around Evie, both of them grinning. Evie and Kahurangi didn't look much alike, except in stature, but their souls had been the same. They'd never had much, but Kahurangi had done her best and often sacrificed her own wants for her daughter. She'd been all the *whanau*, or family, Evie had. Now, she was alone.

"E aroha no ahau ki a koe, e Mama," Evie murmured. *I love you, Mum.*

Next to the photograph, she placed her scuffed hardcover edition of *The Little Match Girl.* She'd read it tomorrow. Finally, she lay down, palms resting on her stomach, and closed her eyes. Almost immediately, unwelcome doubts crept up on her, weighing heavily on her chest, making it difficult to breathe.

Sitting up, she rubbed circles over her heart and focused on the photograph of her mother. Kahurangi had never battled with restlessness the way Evie did, or with knowing where she belonged. She'd been happy here in Itirangi, and she hadn't understood Evie's desire to travel and educate herself about the world. Evie had thought her shortsighted, but now she questioned that. She'd been to half a dozen countries, worked dozens of different jobs, and she'd delighted in her lifestyle for a while, but it no longer held joy. Maybe Kahurangi had known more than her willful daughter thought.

"Oh, Mama," she sighed. "What am I going to do?"

~

DAVY HAD EXPECTED Evelyn to join him in the living area once she'd dressed, but half an hour passed with no sign of her. Was she hiding? It hardly seemed like her usual modus operandi—which as far as he could tell was to flaunt herself in front of him at every opportunity and show him what he'd missed out on—but he didn't question her absence too much. Having some distance from her was a relief after how he'd reacted earlier. He'd never stopped being attracted to Evelyn —any man with a pulse would appreciate the way she looked —but he'd rather she didn't know how she affected him. Not after all this time.

Affixing a wreath to the wall, he eyed his laptop, which waited on the dining table. Sighing, he rubbed his temples, then took a seat in front it, staring at the rows and columns. Numbers and words shifted beneath his gaze, rearranging themselves into gibberish. He gritted his teeth and used his palm to cover all of the columns but one to reduce the distractions. He'd been battling to make sense of the damn spreadsheet all day and was getting nowhere. Dyslexia was a bitch.

Scrolling through the numbers one by one, he tallied them on a calculator. Then two of the rows appeared to swap places and he lost track of where he was. Swearing wholeheartedly, he cleared the calculator and started again. This time, he made it to the end of the column, but even while his mind cheered at the success, his heart sank at the thought of how long it would take to get everything up to date. He had a long way to go.

He grabbed a pen and paper to record the final number, but as he did his attention wavered and the words and numbers became indecipherable again.

"Bollocks!" he growled, hurling the notepad across the room. It dislodged the wreath he'd just hung, which hit the floor with a thud. He hauled in several deep breaths, trying to calm himself. The more stressed he became, the worse his dyslexia got.

"Are you okay?" Evelyn asked, hovering in the doorway. "I heard a bang."

"That was me," he drawled. "Because a grown man is entitled to a temper tantrum sometimes."

To his surprise, she crossed to his side and looked over his shoulder. "What's got you so wound up?" She scanned the screen. "The books for the bar?"

He desperately wanted to slam the laptop shut and chase her away. It was bad enough that he was failing to take care of his business's finances, but to have her witness his shortcoming—well, it wouldn't do.

"Yeah," he muttered, twisting to face her, hoping to draw her attention away from the messy spreadsheet. "I thought you were gonna hide all night."

Annoyance flickered through her eyes as his verbal jab struck true. "I wasn't hiding. I was trying not to intrude. But *you're* hiding something. Tell me what the problem is. It might shock you, but I'm a pretty competent bookkeeper."

He stared, wide-eyed. He couldn't help it. It wasn't that he'd ever thought Evelyn was stupid, but in high school you'd be far more likely to have encountered her at a rave than a library. His thoughts must have shown on his face, because she huffed.

"Don't look at me like that. I'm not dumb."

"Didn't say you were, darlin'," he replied, knowing the endearment would piss her off. "Go ahead, then. Take a look." It couldn't hurt to have a second set of eyes check his figures. He slid the laptop in front of her, and she sat.

"These are a mess," she murmured, scrolling down the page while he watched, enthralled. Not only did she seem to understand the blasted numbers and words, but with a few clicks, she transported the data into a tidy table that most people would have found easy to interpret. She'd been right, she was completely competent, a fact that served to remind him of his own incompetency.

A tangled mash of guilt and shame churned in his gut. Guilt that he'd misjudged her, and shame that his brain was so broken he'd studied the numbers for hours and been unable to do what she had in a matter of minutes.

Finally, she paused, placing her hands one on top of the other and meeting his gaze. "Who taught you to bookkeep?"

He shifted uncomfortably. "Nobody. I muddled my way through it."

"Oh." She winced. "Sorry if I was blunt."

"That's okay." He scratched the back of his neck. "I know they're not great." That tended to happen when a person couldn't tell an "A" from an "N" or a "5" from a "6". He sighed. "I have an audit soon, and they're going to have a field day when they see these."

Her eyes twinkled, and her lips quirked up at the corners. "I see an opportunity here. You let me stay the night, and in return, I'll tidy up your books."

He hesitated, not sure she realized exactly how much work would be involved, and she mistook his hesitation for reluctance.

"I'll keep out of your way," she assured him. "I'm sure you have family plans for Christmas that don't involve me."

"I do have plans," he admitted. His family weren't the kind of people to be bothered by having extra guests, but he wasn't quite sure how he felt about her being near them. It struck a little close to home when he'd once dreamed of her joining their ranks. But he'd also never find someone else willing to bail him out without charging thousands of dollars. "But yeah, you've got yourself a deal."

"Great." She grinned. "Then we'll be even." She paused, then added, "Perhaps I shouldn't admit it, but I'm looking forward to digging into these. I love a good challenge, and it's a well-timed distraction."

He felt compelled to defend his poor bookkeeping skills, but without admitting his condition, he really couldn't, and he didn't want gorgeous Evelyn to know his secret. "I hope you enjoy it, then."

Her gaze softened. "Thanks, Davy. For letting me stay here, and for not calling the girls. I just don't think I can handle being around them right now."

More than anything, he wanted to know why that was, but she didn't volunteer the information and he didn't ask. Evelyn wasn't his business anymore. She'd made that perfectly clear when she'd stuck a knife in his heart and driven away without a care for the shambles of a man she'd left behind.

3

---

vie texted Monica to tell her about the change of plans, then dived happily into Davy's financial records, pleased to have both something to occupy her time and the chance to pay him back. It had been months since she'd challenged her brain with anything more than basic sums at the cafe counter, or the daily sudoku in the newspaper, and she'd been looking for something to test her limits.

She bored easily, which was one of the reasons she constantly tried new jobs, learnt new skills, met new people, and moved to new places. At least, it had been until the constant rotation of people and places itself became dull and unfulfilling.

Seriously, though. These records were in poor condition. She could only decipher as much as she had because she'd spent a lot of time poring over haphazard data before.

Davy returned from making two cups of tea in the squared off kitchen in the corner and dropped into the seat beside her.

"Is there a reason you don't use a software program to manage your information?" she asked.

He scowled. "I prefer to keep it simple. It's a small business, there's no point in spending money on a fancy electronic system."

It may be a small business, but based on the financials, he was making a tidy profit. "You should be able to afford a basic system," she said. "Do you have any other records I need to see?"

"I have papers in my office, but everything has been copied onto the computer. I can get the originals if you need."

"I'll let you know if I do, but for now this should be enough." She stood, shuffling the papers into a pile on the laptop keyboard. "I'll take these back to the bedroom, so I'm out of your hair."

"Suit yourself. And thank you for your help."

"Oh." She deflated. "You're welcome." For some reason, she'd been hoping he'd ask her to stay in the living area so they could work through the documents together. Silly, but she was disappointed he didn't want to keep her company. "Okay then. I'll see you later." With that, she retreated to the bedroom.

Sitting cross-legged on the bed, she began to organize the numbers, cross-checking when they didn't seem to add up. Realizing that in some instances the numbers had been reversed, she frowned. Davy may be a sloppy bookkeeper, but he hadn't struck her as careless. As a teenager, he'd been one of the most conscientious people she knew.

Extending her legs, she reclined against the wall and scratched her chin. She'd have to get the original documentation so she could see which numbers were correct and which were mistakes. Fortunately, this only added to the challenge and gave her a reason to talk to him again. She wandered back to the terribly festive living room. She'd only glanced in as she'd passed earlier, and had been too distracted to fully appreciate the extent of Davy's Christmas-mania, but now she paused and took it all in.

Tinsel adorned every flat surface and lights were strung up on the walls. A number of wreaths were fixed in place, and an eight-foot-tall pine tree stood proudly in the corner with a selection of gift-wrapped boxes beneath it, surrounded by fake snow. The tree itself was only partially decorated. A work in progress. Davy hung a red ball from the end of a branch and turned to smile at her. It was an easy, toothy smile. The kind you might give a close friend. The kind that had no business making her heart flutter.

"How's it going?" he asked.

Evie debated how to phrase this diplomatically. She decided the direct approach would be best. "Not all of the numbers match. Can I get those papers you mentioned to cross-check with the spreadsheet?"

He raked a hand through his hair, tousling the ginger locks, which stood up like he'd been electrocuted. "Man, it's worse than I thought. Are you sure?"

"I'm sure," she replied. "But it's not a big deal if you keep all your paperwork."

He looked pained. "I do. I'll get it for you."

She hesitated, then asked, "Would you like me to show you what kind of errors I'm talking about? I don't want to go ahead and change anything if I'm going to screw up your record-keeping system."

THE BAUBLE CLUTCHED in Davy's fist shattered, shards digging into his skin.

"No," he snapped, hating the way she flinched back from him. "You don't need to show me. I believe you."

She persisted. "I know I agreed to tidy your books, but the decisions on how to do that are still yours." She opened the laptop on the coffee table, hit a few keys, then beckoned him over.

With a sense of impending doom, he crossed to her side and pretended to read over her shoulder. He nodded, as if it made sense. In reality, the letters were circling and spinning before his eyes. She pointed to a column and explained how she'd determined where the issues had arisen. Her words may as well have been gobbledygook.

Finally, she leveled him with an irritated glare. "Have you listened to anything I've said?"

"Abso-friggin-lutely," he exclaimed, trying so hard to sound enthusiastic that it came out sarcastic. "I mean, of course."

"I highly doubt that. What's one thing I've said in the last few minutes?" When he couldn't reply, she stood abruptly. "If you don't care about the details, just say so next time."

He grabbed her shoulder. "Wait."

She froze. Then, very deliberately, she lifted his hand off her shoulder and stepped out of reach. "What?"

He swallowed, his tongue thick. He had to come clean and hope she didn't laugh at him.

"I'm dyslexic," he admitted. "I can't understand what you're trying to show me, because I can't read it." He hung his head, studied the floor, and waited for her scorn. After all, what grown-ass man couldn't read properly?

But she didn't laugh. Instead, she ordered him to look at her. He lifted his gaze slowly.

"Why didn't you tell me that at the beginning?" she asked, her tone gentle.

He shrugged. "I was embarrassed. Wouldn't you be?"

Her brows drew together. "How did I not notice this when we were dating?"

He shrugged again. "I have lots of coping mechanisms, but sometimes it isn't enough. Some days I can manage, and some days I'm practically illiterate. It's pathetic."

Evie held eye contact and enunciated clearly, "Some people are good at some things, and some are good at others.

Reading isn't your strong suit. That's not the end of the world. As far as your records go, you'll just have to trust me, or get a second opinion."

"I trust you." He had to. No one else had ever seen the state of his records, and he'd prefer to keep it that way for as long as he could. He supposed that meant until the auditor arrived. Even the thought unsettled his stomach. He pushed it from his mind and instead pondered the mystery of Evelyn. When it came to his financial records, she seemed to genuinely know what she was doing—and enjoyed it. Weird, that. He'd never have picked her as the type of person who liked math, and he'd thought he'd known her well. Now, he wondered how much of what he knew was true and how much was his own preconception. After all, she'd thought she'd known him, too, but he'd kept his condition from her.

"How long are you staying in the area?" he asked. "This might take a while longer than you thought."

She nibbled her lower lip. "I really don't know."

He nodded. It wouldn't be the first time Evelyn blew through town with no clue where she was going or what she was doing next. She seemed to prefer living that way. A fact that rankled when he'd once hoped for her to settle down with him.

"If it convinces you to stay longer, I'll pay you for your time." Heck, she could name her price.

She rolled her eyes. "I said I'd do it, so I'll do it. I should be in Timaru for at least a week, which gives me plenty of time. A friend of mine runs an orchard and I'll be berry picking for her over New Year's. I can work on your books in the evenings. After I've gotten the old data up to scratch, you're on your own for anything going forward. Deal?"

"Deal," he replied without hesitation, shaking the hand she extended. Then, overwhelmed by a surge of gratitude, he ducked his head and kissed her cheek.

She backed up so quickly it would have been comical if

not for the blow to his ego, as effective as a karate chop to the throat. "Don't do that." Her voice was shaky.

He held up his hands in a gesture of peace. "Sorry, sorry. I got carried away."

"Yes, you did."

He winced. She wasn't letting his faux pas go without comment.

"Don't do it again," she said. "If you need me, I'll be in the bedroom. You can bring your paperwork to me there. It's more comfortable."

The way she said that made him think physical comfort wasn't the only thing on her mind. Had his kiss made her uncomfortable? He never wanted to be one of those men who made women nervous. He'd seen plenty of those guys at his bar over the years and ejected them as rapidly as possible. But maybe it wasn't that. Maybe the past between them made her uncomfortable. If so, he wasn't doing a damn thing to make it easier for her. She'd crushed him, so it was only fair she feel a little of what he had.

She took the laptop and left. He rubbed his eyelids, strolled to the sofa and slumped onto it. This was not how he'd thought he'd be spending Christmas Eve.

4

Once Davy had delivered his papers, Evie perched the computer on her lap and opened a second spreadsheet. She labeled a series of worksheets and columns, and started importing data from one file to the other, matching items up to the receipts and invoices stacked beside her. As the rows of numbers morphed into a meaningful pattern, she smiled in satisfaction.

At least, she did until Christmas music blared through the crack beneath the door.

Grinding her teeth together, she ignored the festive beat. Or tried to, anyway. When Davy cranked the volume, she slapped her hands over her ears to muffle the obnoxious noise, but they did nothing to soften the drone of his voice when he began to sing.

"Tis the season to be jolly, fa-la-la-la-la."

He practically yelled the lyrics. Was he actually crazy, or was he trying to rile her? If so, she couldn't fathom why. God knew she deserved a little torture for dropping him like a hot potato the way she had, but surely revenge should take a back seat to keeping her on side until she'd gotten his books in shape. Besides, she'd thought they'd reached a truce.

Focusing on the screen, she strove, unsuccessfully, to tune out the Irishman's boisterous singing. She endured it for several minutes, then set the laptop aside and stomped down the hall to the living room, throwing the door open.

"Turn down the racket," she hollered.

Davy tapped his ear and shrugged, indicating that he couldn't hear her. His shit-eating grin said otherwise.

"Shut it off," she insisted, and mimed rotating the volume dial.

His grin widened, and he repeated the movement.

"Shut up!" she roared at the exact moment he reached over and dialed down the music to a pleasant background noise.

His wide green eyes feigned shock. "No need to shout at me, Evelyn. I'm not a mind reader. How can I help you?"

For the first time, she noticed the scarf of tinsel wrapped around his neck and the sparkly green baubles he clasped. "Are those leprechaun testicles?"

Davy just stared at her for the length of a heartbeat, then he guffawed. "Leprechaun balls," he choked. "That's a new one."

She scowled to hide the flicker of interest aroused by his smile. "That's what they look like."

He raised one ginger eyebrow. "Am I detecting some Grinchy vibes coming from my house guest? Are you a Christmas Grinch, Miss Parata? I'd never have thought it of you. You're the life of the party."

Ah, yes. There it was. Someone expecting her to be her usual perky self, exactly as she'd feared would happen. Sighing, she scrubbed a hand down her face. "I can't always be 'on', Davy. Sometimes even the life of the party needs a bit of down time."

His expression turned curious. "Of course you do. Just took me by surprise, is all. Here." He passed her one of the green baubles. "Put this on the tree. Decorating works wonders for mood."

She looked at the bauble as if it were a viper, then she glanced at the tree, wondering where he expected her to hang it. The tree was so beautifully decorated it could have a full page spread in *Interior Design: The Christmas Edition*, and she was a total amateur. She couldn't help but feel that whatever she did, she'd ruin its perfect symmetry.

With a shake of her head, she tossed it back at him. "Don't be ridiculous. You do it."

He frowned at her, crossing his forearms over his plaid-clad chest. "Are you *scared* to decorate my tree?"

She scoffed. "I'm not scared of anything. I just don't *do* Christmas. At least not the way you do. I have my own traditions and they don't involve glittery leprechaun testicles."

"You know what? I think you're scared. As a matter of fact, I think you're too chicken-shit to hang this bauble," he held it up by the twine loop, "from that branch." He pointed to an empty pine twig. "If you're not, prove me wrong." He leaned forward, smirking. "I *dare* you."

If he'd phrased it differently, she could have taken the high ground, but she couldn't turn down a dare, and he knew it. She snatched the ball from his grip and threaded it onto the branch.

"There. Happy?"

"Thrilled."

He looked it too, damn him.

"If you hang another five decorations, I'll turn down the music so you can carry on in true Grinch style."

Her hands went to her hips. "I can't believe you're holding the volume control hostage."

"Believe it, girl. You'd better get your A into G."

"Fine." She reached into the box of decorations and grabbed the first one she touched. It almost crumpled beneath her thumb and she softened her hold on it. The paper sides of a handmade cube were colored alternately red and green by what looked like the enthusiastic hand of a child with a felt-tip pen. One side was smooth and glossy. A photograph. Lifting the cube, she peered at the photo, which had been faded by years of wear and tear. It showed a little boy with a messy head of straw-like hair and a smattering of freckles.

"Is this you?" she asked, touching the miniature face.

"Yes," he said, far nearer than she'd thought he was. If she turned, her nose might brush his chest. "That was taken back in Ireland, before we moved here. We made decorations each Christmas, and Mam kept them all, bless her hoarder's soul. She gave them to me a few years ago."

Something stung Evie's eyes and she blinked, swallowing against the tightness in her throat. She would *not* get emotional at the thought of little Davy making this terrible decoration, or of his mother saving it all these years, even though it had crossed an ocean. She would most definitely not wallow in self-pity because all her own mum had left for her was a photograph and a tragic storybook. She was made of tougher stuff than that.

"Sweet," she said, and handed it to him, choosing a selection of mass-produced baubles instead. She didn't need any more cutesy stories.

Deciding it was easier to dive in than worry about ruining the aesthetic, she placed three baubles in quick succession and was stretching onto her toes to hang the fourth when Davy's torso brushed her back and he plucked it from her fingers, putting it on the branch she'd been aiming for.

"Where do you want the last one?" he asked.

She hung it on the lowest level of the tree. "There. Can you turn it down now?"

"I promised, didn't I?"

. . .

After an hour and a half of blessed quiet, a rumbling stomach drove Evie from the bedroom. She needed food, ASAP. There was no sign of Davy, so she wandered to the kitchen and searched the cupboards for a bowl and a box of cereal. There was nothing like breakfast for dinner. She poured a healthy serving of cocoa pops and was splashing them with milk when footsteps padded down the hall and Davy came into view, naked except for a towel slung low over his hips.

Evie's breath hitched. She hadn't seen this much of him since they were seventeen and she'd hoped he could be her forever boy. They could've traveled the world together for the rest of their lives, a dream she'd never expressed to him, especially after she found out how attached to Itirangi he was.

Her gaze roved over him. His skin had the same milky coloring as before, and the dusting of hair on his chest contrasted sharply, orange on white. He'd filled out in the intervening years, his torso blocky and shoulders wide. He'd been a lanky teenager, with all the height of a man but none of the stature. At some point, that had changed. He'd aged well.

Breath eased from between his parted lips and his eyes locked on hers. To her surprise, no snappy quip was forthcoming on either side of the stare-down. Flecks of emerald sparkled in the mossy green of his irises, and she watched them, mesmerized. Her heart pitter-pattered against the inside of her ribcage like it was trying to break free.

A loud beeping interrupted the moment, drawing her attention to the fridge, which she'd left open. She hurried over, slotted the milk bottle into the door, and closed it. Then she grabbed the bowl of cocoa pops and sat at the dining table, spooning a mound of the crackling cereal into her mouth.

"Cereal for dinner?" he asked, making no move to cover himself.

"Yeah. You got a problem with that?"

He winked. *Winked.* The cheeky devil. "Not if you make me some, too."

Because she was taking advantage of his hospitality, she could hardly say no. Smiling merrily, he pulled out the chair opposite her while she returned to the kitchen area and heaped cocoa pops into a second bowl, drowning them in full-fat milk. Then she passed them to him, taking pains not to touch his bare skin, before she settled back and continued to eat her own.

"Thank you, kind-hearted lady," he drawled, looking pleased with himself as he started on the cereal. She recalled him looking exactly the same way after the first time they'd had sex, and her heart sped at the memory. Already, the nearness of his half-naked body had her hormones on high alert. She had a sixth sense for sexy guys, and Davy set off her internal hotness radar something wicked.

What did it mean that after all this time and distance she still wanted to jump his bones? Every other man she'd been with, she'd happily banged out of her system. If she encountered them now, she might consider a good romp for old time's sake, but she knew without an ounce of doubt that her palms wouldn't sweat and her thighs wouldn't clench the way they did now.

Had she been a fool to leave him? At eighteen, with grand ideas about the adventures awaiting her in the world outside Itirangi, she'd believed with all her heart that she'd be a fool to stay. She didn't regret the way her life had turned out, but now she wondered if she'd been naïve to think she could have the same connection with other men.

"Earth to Evelyn. You in there?"

Her head snapped up, and she hoped her thoughts weren't written on her face. "Yes, just thinking."

He cocked his head and set his spoon aside. "About what?"

"Nothing interesting."

He leaned forward, one elbow on the table, chin resting on his palm. "And how do you know what I'd find interesting?"

She held his gaze. "Because I used to know you, and trust me when I say you should stop asking." Mulling over their break-up would do neither of them any good. She'd hurt him—badly—and she didn't want to reopen old wounds. His, or hers.

To his credit, he didn't pursue the line of questioning. Maybe he realized she was only being honest. As she rinsed her cereal bowl and stacked it away, she wondered whether he'd dated much over the years. While she'd always wanted him to be happy, she found she didn't like the idea of him seeing other women. She liked to think Aria or Sophie would have told her if there'd been someone in the picture, but then Evie had never let on how serious they'd been about each other as kids. They had no idea how deep her feelings for him had gone. Not even her reluctance to go to his bar hadn't tipped them off. They'd put it down to a disdain for small-town venues, and she'd let them believe it. If they knew one-tenth of the tangle of emotions that sprang up inside her each time she saw him, they'd have tried to push the two of them together long before now.

No, it was best for everyone involved that they'd kept things on the down low.

She bid him goodnight and decided not to leave her bedroom again for the evening. She could survive Christmas without seeing much of him at all.

She had to, for her own peace of mind.

Davy lay in bed, uncomfortably hard. Having Evelyn just down the hall, where he could envision her in tiny summer pajamas, drove him out of his mind. He wasn't alone in his lust, either. He'd seen the way she'd ogled him. Though she wouldn't admit it, she was attracted to him, and that knowledge both satisfied and relieved him. Regardless of the heartbreak she'd heaped on him when they were young, he still wanted her, and thank-frigging-God she felt the same way. One-sided attraction wasn't something to be recommended.

Closing his eyes, he thought of the last time he'd seen her before today. It had been the day of Aria's wedding, and Evelyn had been a bridesmaid, resplendent in a figure-hugging gold dress. She'd sung at the ceremony, and taken his breath away. She'd always liked to sing, but he'd forgotten how moving it could be. How her raw, throaty voice could wrap around him like a blanket and make him shiver with delight. He'd hoped to talk to her, and try to put some of the awkwardness of the past years behind them, perhaps start fresh, but she'd stayed on the dance floor all night, and seemed to dance with every man except him. He'd drunk himself under the bar—which took a fair amount of effort—and by the time he'd recovered enough to make it to the wedding breakfast, she was gone.

Now she was a guest in his home, trusting him to give her safe shelter for Christmas. Much as he may want to, he wasn't going to abuse that trust by doing anything inappropriate. If only his body would get the message that she was off limits. Rolling over, he imagined jumping into the frigid water of Lake Itirangi, hoping to cool his ardor. It was going to be a long night.

---

5

*D*avy woke early, stretched toward the ceiling, and smiled.

Christmas Day. How he loved it.

He checked his watch, noting that his family would arrive in a few hours for lunch, so he needed to start preparing the food. His mouth watered at the thought of their traditional Christmas fare—roast turkey, baked ham, cranberry sauce, carrots, parsnips, and a scrumptious trifle for dessert.

His stomach grumbled and he rubbed the flat surface of his belly. Food would come later. First, coffee. Without bothering to dress, he padded next door, into the kitchen and dining area, where he stopped dead in his tracks.

Shit, damn, hell.

He'd forgotten he had a guest. And apparently, she was an early riser. She stood in front of the kitchen counter, balanced on one leg, her foot on a thin yoga mat and an arm pointed out in front of her. Her other arm and leg were bowed above her body so that she looked like a ballerina paused midway through a dance. He expected her to shriek at the sight of him, but she didn't react at all. He looked closer and realized her eyes were shut. She didn't know he was there.

Feeling like a pervert, but too entranced to leave, he admired her form, both in terms of her yoga technique and her figure. She was effortlessly graceful, like she'd been doing this her whole life. She didn't teeter or move so much as an eyelash. Every muscle remained perfectly still. He'd never seen anyone so serene, certainly not Evelyn.

Her legs, though short, were shapely, her thighs curved into a rounded bottom that gave way to a slim torso and heart-stoppingly perfect breasts, which he knew from experience could not be contained by a man's hands. Those breasts had been enough to reduce him to a slathering mess as a boy.

Her neck was long and elegant, her chin pointed, and cheekbones pronounced. His gaze wandered leisurely back down to her feet, which were ridiculously tiny. He recalled that her hands were also small. He'd burst with pride back when she'd put her two delicate hands side by side along his shaft and not fully encompassed him.

Something thumped his pelvis. Glancing down, he realized he had an erection. Also, he was naked, and watching Evelyn like a creep.

"Feck," he swore.

Her eyes opened. In about two seconds, she took in his nudity and dropped from her position into a crouch, brandishing her miniature fists at him. When she didn't scream, he had to wonder how common it was for horny men to disrupt her yoga routine with unwanted advances.

"What the hell are you doing?" she demanded, fixing him with a psycho glare that threatened all kinds of painful revenge if he didn't back off immediately.

"I'm so sorry." He lowered his hands to cover his junk, and edged away, reluctant to turn his back lest she either attack, or be blinded by the stunning white glow of his ass.

Once in the hall, he darted to his bedroom and threw on black jeans and a snug green t-shirt. Properly attired, he hurried back, intent on making amends.

In the doorway, he bumped into the rolled-up end of Evelyn's yoga mat. Or had she hit him with it? At this point, he wasn't sure, and he couldn't blame her if she had.

"I'm so sorry about that," he told her again. "I forgot you were here. Normally I can walk around in the buff and there's no one to see. I swear to Mother Mary, I didn't mean to shock you like that."

Her brow furrowed, and she glanced from him to the yoga mat, as if considering whether to whack him over the head with it. He wouldn't stop her. He deserved it.

"Are you even Catholic?" she asked.

He grinned. She'd opted not to hurt him yet. "My Mam would have my head if I said no."

She rolled her eyes. "But do you go to church?"

"Once or twice a year, when Mam gets concerned about the wellbeing of my immortal soul. I can recite 'Our Father', 'Hail Mary', and 'Glory Be' word for word, like any good Irish boy."

"Of course you can," she muttered, like his revelation explained everything. "Are you going to let me past? Or do I need to knee you in the nads?" She tried to step around him, but he shuffled over and blocked her path. She raised her left knee menacingly.

"No need to maim me. I'll let you pass as soon as you tell me why in God's name you were exercising at the ass-crack of dawn on Christmas morning. It's a day for sleeping late and eating too much, not working on your bikini body."

She shoved his shoulders. He backed up a little, knowing she could push him with all her strength and not move him thanks to years of playing lock on the rugby field, but he wouldn't use his physicality to intimidate her.

"I do yoga every day," she said as she brushed past him. "Christmas is no different. It's a day like any other."

"No it's not," he called after her. "It's a holiday. Meant to be enjoyed."

"So?" She paused in the doorway of the spare bedroom. "I *enjoy* yoga. And don't be judgey, Irishman. I have Christmas traditions, too. Mine are different from yours, but that doesn't make them any less valid."

"Touché." She had him there. Who was he to decide what was and wasn't an appropriate way to spend Christmas?

EVIE PACKED her yoga mat away and showered to rinse off the fine sheen of sweat left over from her routine. Though it was cool inside, when she peeped between the curtains, the sky was a vivid blue with fluffy clouds drifting across it. She dressed in one of her favorite scoop-necked tops and a skort —a pair of shorts with a wrap-around front that had the overall effect of resembling a skirt.

Opening the window, she leaned out and breathed in the fresh air. At this height, she could see clear over the surrounding buildings and down to the lake. It was too early for anyone to be up and about except for a lone woman jogging along the lake shore. The temperature was mild and pleasant, but the glorious summer sky promised a scorcher of a day to come.

From her suitcase, she grabbed a box of herbal tea and strode to the kitchen, determined to rescue her mood. As she entered the dining area, Davy's broad back came into view. He stood at the counter, spreading cream cheese on bagels before smothering raspberry jam on top. When she flicked the kettle on, he handed her one.

"Eat up."

"Thanks." The simple gesture touched her heart. Other

than her mother and one or two of her closest friends, no one had ever cooked for her. Certainly not any man.

Calm down, she told herself. *It's a bagel, not a declaration of undying affection.*

Christmas carols played softly in the background. The kettle boiled and she poured hot water into a teacup, watching as pink diffused from the tea bag into the drink.

"My family is coming by for lunch," Davy told her as he rinsed and dried a turkey. "It's a tradition for us. Have a big lunch, then munch on leftovers all day."

"I'll leave," she said, tossing out the tea bag and taking her breakfast to the table. "Get out of the way. Let you guys enjoy your lunch."

"Don't be silly. It's Christmas. You're welcome to join us."

She nibbled on her lip, hesitant. "I don't want to intrude." She paused, thinking about how she didn't actually have anywhere else to go, other than for a long walk around town. This was a large apartment, with plenty of room—she could stay out of the way. "Perhaps I could hang out in the bedroom and keep myself busy?"

He glanced up, looking dubious. "If that's what you'd prefer, but think on it. We're a family who firmly believes in the more, the merrier."

She nodded, and finished her bagel and tea in silence while he mixed stuffing and shoved it into the turkey. "Thanks for the breakfast," she said, getting up to wash and dry the plate.

"No problem."

Back in the bedroom, she opened her ten-dollar bottle of wine and half-filled the teacup she'd brought with her, taking a sip and savoring the tingle on her tongue. Sparkling Moscato may be cheap, but it was her favorite. In her opinion, no hundred-year-old, pricey vintage could compete, although many of her friends disagreed. Clarissa, in particular, was a connoisseur.

The photo of her mother faced her from the bedside cabinet. Evie glanced away, unable to look at it for long. She grabbed a donut from the plastic carton stored in her suitcase and bit into it, loving the flakiness of the outside and the softness of the center. Cinnamon sugar coated her fingers and she licked them. *Bliss.*

She didn't need an over-the-top Christmas celebration. All she needed was this: wine, donuts, *The Little Match Girl,* and her mum.

Mum.

A tear welled up and slid over one cheek. Another followed. It didn't matter that she was upholding their traditions—Kahurangi was gone, and Evie didn't want to spend Christmas without her. Her soul ached with loneliness. Her heart hurt from it. She remembered her mother saying, year after year, "We may not have fancy gifts, but we'll always have each other, tamahine." But they didn't, not anymore, because she'd died and left Evie on her own.

This time last year, Kahurangi had been bedridden, and fading fast. Her skin had been unusually colorless, her energy low as her body used whatever supplies it possessed to fight the cancer. She'd known she was dying, but Evie denied it, preferring to cling to the hope of a Christmas miracle. Surely they deserved one after all they'd been through together. But no miracle came, and Kahurangi passed away days later.

Evie's tears flowed quickly, streaming down her face and dripping off her chin. She pushed the donuts away and clutched the book to her, rocking back and forth. A sob tore from deep in her chest. A miserable, bitter sound she couldn't contain.

It wasn't fair. Her mum hadn't even been fifty. She'd exercised regularly, not smoked, and watched what she ate. Why had the universe stolen her away?

Why had there been nothing Evie could do to stop it?

She'd wondered, so many times, whether her mum would

be alive if only they'd caught the cancer earlier, or been able to afford a new treatment on the market. Sniffling, she wiped her leaky eyes on the bed sheet. *Coulda, woulda, shoulda.* None of that meant anything now. Kahurangi had died and left her alone for all the Christmases to come.

The tears started anew, and she cursed herself for being pathetic. She'd thought she'd finished crying months ago. But then, maybe her mother wasn't the only reason for her tears. Maybe the stress of the last two days had caught up with her. In the end, it didn't really matter *why* she was crying. What mattered was that she was without family on Christmas Day, for the first time ever.

6

With the turkey and ham in the oven, Davy turned his attention to the vegetables and sauce. Heavy Christmas meals weren't *de rigueur* in New Zealand because Christmas happened during midsummer, but his Irish family erred toward the traditions of the homeland. They loved New Zealand, but that didn't stop his Mam from missing cold Christmases in Ireland.

As he began to peel parsnips, his playlist ended. He went to his phone, selected a new playlist, and was about to start the music when a strange high-pitched keening noise caught his attention. Frowning, he followed the sound into the hall. It was coming from the room Evelyn had claimed. Perhaps she was playing her own music.

But no, if she'd had her own sound system, she would have used it to drown out his Christmas carols.

Pausing outside the door, he put his ear to the wood and listened. The keening had stopped, but now he heard watery blubbering. Hell, she was crying. Absolutely bawling, if his ears could be believed.

What had he done? She hadn't seemed upset with him during breakfast, but perhaps she'd taken his unwelcome and unexpected nudity harder than he'd thought. Could it be that he'd frightened her? God, he hoped not.

He chewed on his tongue. Dare he open the door?

If he'd truly upset her, he should make it right. But if this was his fault, wouldn't he be doing her a favor by staying away?

Suck it up, boyo. Do the right thing.

Maybe it wasn't anything he'd done. Maybe this was about her mother. He laid a palm against the door, reluctant to bust in on her, but with any other woman, he'd have entered already. He shouldn't treat Evelyn differently because of their past. So thinking, he pushed the door open and peered around. She sat cross-legged on the bed, clutching a hardback book, a half-drunk glass of wine on the nightstand and a six-pack of donuts beside her. She looked up, and the miserable expression in her puffy red eyes hit him like a knife in the gut. Yeah, she was upset about far more than something stupid he'd done. This was raw grief.

"Go away," she moaned, shutting her eyes as though she couldn't bear to look at him. "Leave me be."

He stepped cautiously into the room, his attention focused entirely on her. "I'm sorry. I can't do that, Evelyn. Not when you're hurting like this."

"I don't need your pity," she mumbled, studying her hands.

He felt utterly useless. This was Evelyn. Usually flirtatious, always maddening, never one to dwell on the negatives. He wasn't equipped to see her this way. He watched her dab her eyes with a fingertip, shoulders hunched. She drew her knees to her chest and hugged them, her gaze flickering to something on the nightstand. Davy crossed to her side, perched on the edge of the bed, and put an arm around her.

She didn't shrug him off, which was telling in and of itself. From here, he could see the photograph displayed in a scarred wooden frame. It was of Evelyn and her mother.

Sympathy twisted a knot in his gut. The women had always been close, and losing her must have been far more difficult than Evelyn ever let on.

"There, there," he said awkwardly, stroking her silky hair. "Let it out. It will be okay."

"You don't know that," she whispered, then screwed up her face as she realized she'd shown weakness, not something she'd ever enjoyed. "You can go. I'm fine."

Davy didn't budge. "You'll have to be more convincing than that."

She shook her shoulders, dislodging his arm, then took a deep, uneven breath, dried her eyes on the sheet, and bared her teeth in a semblance of a smile. "I'm okay," she said. "Completely fine."

Welp, he was convinced. Convinced that she was anything but fine. He took her hand. "Sweetheart, please let me help. I know I'm probably not who you want to be with right now, but unless you want me to call Sophie or Aria, I'm who you've got."

She sniffed. "Don't call the girls. I just need…" She trailed off. "I don't know."

"How about you come and help me prepare lunch," he suggested, rubbing his thumb across the back of her hand. "I know it's not exciting, but it might take your mind off things. Then you can stay and eat with us."

She groaned and covered her face with her free hand. "I don't know if I can handle being social right now. Why would you even want me intruding on your family lunch? Won't they think it's weird?"

He understood her hesitation. Though they'd dated in high school, she'd never met his parents, despite his wishes to the contrary. Meeting the parents had been "a little too real" for teenage Evelyn.

Yeah, that had stung.

He shrugged. "My family won't mind a bit. They'd love to

have company, and you aren't just some random person. You're you."

She huffed, reclaimed her hand, and hugged her knees again. "Why do you call me that?"

He paused, caught off guard. "Evelyn? It's your name, isn't it?"

"Yeah, but nobody besides Mum ever used it. To everyone else, I'm just Evie."

"I like the way 'Evelyn' sounds," he said. "It's a nice name. And you're not 'just' anything. You're beautiful and smart and intriguing, but I guess you already know that."

"Never hurts to hear someone say it," she replied, a ghost of a grin on her face. "Okay, I'll join your lunch. I appreciate you inviting me."

"You're very welcome." He stood, offered her a hand, and hauled her to her feet.

"Thank you," she whispered, eyes glimmering with the remnants of tears. "For being so nice to me. I know it can't be easy." Then, to his complete astonishment, she planted a kiss on him. It was over nearly as soon as it began and she ducked around him and scurried away. He touched his lips wonderingly.

If he was sensible, he'd want nothing to do with Evelyn. She was the kind of trouble that could break his heart. But damn, she had the softest lips he'd ever kissed.

Why had she kissed him?

Evie's mouth tingled where it had touched Davy's. A mistake. She'd been overcome by gratitude toward him for being so kind, and it had just happened.

On top of that, it seemed she would be joining the O'Connors for lunch. Never mind that she wouldn't add much to the holiday cheer, he seemed almost eager to have her there. While she hadn't appreciated his interfering at first, now she was relieved she'd have something to do other than wallow in grief all day.

"Where are you going?" Davy called after her.

She turned. He stood in the hall, looking baffled. And strangely adorable. Not sexy at all, she reminded herself. For his sake, she couldn't afford to be attracted to him. She didn't want to risk hurting him again just because she didn't know what she wanted out of her life anymore.

"We're making lunch," she reminded him, padding up the carpeted hall to the kitchen and dining area. Heavy footsteps told her he'd followed.

He tapped her shoulder. "What was that?"

She didn't turn. "Nothing. Now let's get cooking. Don't worry, I won't mess anything up. I've worked in a few cafes and restaurants over the years." She put her hands on her hips and surveyed the space. "Where do you want me?"

A pregnant pause came on the heel of her words. She winced. She should have phrased the question differently. Fortunately, he didn't make the obvious joke.

"Can you finish peeling the parsnips and carrots?" he asked, coming around to stand beside her. "I'll focus on the sauce."

"Easy." She grabbed the discarded peeler and set to work. "Is this what an Irish Christmas lunch looks like?"

"Traditionally, the Irish celebrate with Christmas dinner," he said in his pleasant lilting accent as he moved to the stovetop to check the sauce. "We changed it to lunch, but otherwise yes, this is more or less what a traditional Christmas meal would include."

She scanned the kitchen. "Where are the potatoes?"

He grinned. "Believe it or not, we're not all about the potatoes. Although you can't deny, they're a versatile vegetable. They make chips and crisps, you can roast them or bake them, and they're the key ingredient to vodka. Potatoes are a bloody good time."

"Okay, Mr. Potato Head."

"You laugh," he said, grabbing a spoon from a drawer, "but it's true. I challenge you to name one other vegetable you can do all those things with."

Evie thought for a moment, then with a smug grin, replied, "Kumara."

"Aha! Otherwise known as sweet *potato*."

The smile vanished. "Completely different thing."

"One and the same," he countered.

"Does anyone ever tell you how annoying you are?"

"Only when they know I'm right."

She rinsed the parsnips, then turned her attention to the carrots. "How big is your family? Seems like there's enough here to feed a small army."

"Not that big. Just big eaters. There will be four and a half people coming over."

She laughed. "A half?"

Davy laughed with her. "My nephew. He's only two, so I don't think he qualifies as a full person yet."

"That's Angus's kid? He's younger than you, right?"

"He's twenty-two."

Young to have a two-year-old, but old enough to be a good parent. She tried to recall his face. He'd been a kid himself last she'd seen him. Gangly and ginger, with a big mouth and a chip on his shoulder, willing to take on anyone who mocked his hair or accent. Hard to imagine him as a father.

She finished with the carrots at the same time Davy took the sauce off the stove and set it aside to cool. She leaned over the pot and sniffed. It smelled good. Sweet, yet tart.

"What next, Chef?"

"Can you whip some cream for the trifle?" he asked. "It's

in the fridge, and there's vanilla paste and confectioner's sugar in the pantry."

She pulled a face. "I should have known you'd be one of those people who pollutes their cream." Nonetheless, she searched for the ingredients he'd specified. As she reached for the vanilla paste on the top shelf, it struck her that her tears had dried and, however unlikely, she was having a good time.

"Too short, pipsqueak?"

She bounced off the floor and closed her hand around the tube. "I'm Goldilocks," she said, waving her fist in triumph. "Just right, smart ass."

He glanced over his shoulder and down at his backside. "Why, thank you for noticing."

She hid her mouth behind her hand so he couldn't see her smile. "Oh, the gems keep on coming." After emptying the ingredients into a bowl, she searched the cupboards until she found an electric beater, and started it up.

Davy, who'd begun chopping a collection of summer fruit, jerked in surprise. "Give a guy some warning."

She pointed to her ear and mouthed, "I can't hear you."

"Sure you can't."

She shrugged helplessly.

"Evil Evelyn, that's what they should call you." Turning away, he continued dicing fruit. Evie finished whipping the cream and shimmied across the kitchen, bumping him with her hip. She swiped a piece of strawberry, popped it between her lips, and licked the juice from her fingers.

"You sneaky little thief."

She sashayed away and stored the whipped cream in the fridge. "I feel no shame. Custard next?"

"That's right."

They worked in tandem for the next couple of hours, putting lunch together bit by bit, exchanging sarcastic comments as they went. The mood slowly improved, though to be fair, it couldn't have gotten worse than sobbing alone in her ex's spare bedroom on Christmas day.

But then someone knocked on the door, and her stomach plummeted like she'd dropped twenty vertical meters.

"Come in," Davy yelled. "It's open."

Evie heard the swish of the door over carpet and a woman's voice with a thick Irish accent called, "Too busy to greet your Mam, are you, boy?"

"I'm taking care of the holiday meal you're about to enjoy," he said.

"Cheeky boy. I didn't raise you to give me lip." Mrs. O'Connor came around the corner. She had a rigid bearing with good posture and hair that matched her son's, topping out no more than an inch above five feet. Freckles dusted her face, making her cheeks look almost tan, and blue eyes beamed like lasers from beneath hooded lids.

"Oh." She came to a stop, her gaze settling on Evie. "And who might you be?"

Evie immediately rethought her plans to stay for the meal. She didn't belong here. "I'm just le—"

"Evelyn," Davy interrupted, when she'd been about to politely excuse herself. "This is my Mam and Paps." A gray-haired gentleman with bushy brows followed Davy's mother into the room. Behind him came a lanky redhead and a petite Japanese woman with a toddler clinging to her leg. "I think you know Angus," he continued.

"From a very long time ago. He probably doesn't remember me."

Angus's eyes widened in surprise, but he shook his head. "I remember you, Evie. You're kind of hard to forget." He took the Japanese woman's hand. She smiled warmly, her dark eyes twinkling and thin lips curving into a smile. "This is my partner, Mariko, and our son Reo."

"Lovely to meet you," Evie said, and then the entire O'Connor clan watched her curiously, as if waiting for an explanation for her presence. She gave them one. "My car broke down and the mechanic isn't open until tomorrow, so I'm stuck here. Davy and I know each other from school. He let me crash in his spare bedroom. I should say, one of his *many* spare bedrooms. This place is massive."

Davy's father glanced between the two of them, taking in the food stains on their clothing, and the tension in the air. He raised an eyebrow. "A pleasure to meet you, Evelyn." His accent was less pronounced than his wife's. "Call me Hugh. My wife is Eileen."

"Merry Christmas, Hugh." She turned to Davy. "Are you okay to finish lunch?"

He nodded.

Evie smiled at everyone. "If you'll excuse me, I'm going to go clean myself up."

7

"*S*he just happened to break down outside your place, eh?" Angus asked the minute Evelyn left the room.

Davy didn't appreciate his tone. "She did," he said, warning his brother off with a look. The last thing he needed was for their mother to get ideas.

Angus's grin widened. His baby brother had never been able to take a hint. "If I remember correctly—and I usually do—you and Evie dated during high school. Odd that her car would break down outside your bar, of all places. What do you suppose she was doing here?"

Davy shrugged. "Didn't ask. It's none of my business. Wipe that smirk off your face, kid. Evelyn and I went out a handful of times nine years ago, it means nothing that she's here now. It's a small town, that's all."

"You dated that girl?" Eileen asked, overhearing. Her brow crinkled in disbelief. "And I didn't know about it?"

Davy crossed his arms. Angus had done it now. "I don't bring every girl I date home to meet you, Mam."

"Perhaps not, but I'd have thought you'd bring home one as pretty and polite as that," she said tartly.

Yeah, well, he would've, if she'd been inclined to agree.

"Lay off, Eileen," Hugh said. "Give the boy a break. I'm sure you didn't tell Colleen and Willy everything we got up to when we were young."

She blushed, and Angus and Davy stuck their fingers in their ears at the same time.

"We don't need to hear this," Angus said. "Our ears are delicate."

Mariko heaved Reo up and settled him on her slim hip. "Angus, why don't you help Davy bring lunch over? We'll set up the table." While the O'Connors spoke with varying degrees of the Irish accent, Mariko's sweet voice tripped over L's.

"Excellent plan, Mariko," Hugh agreed, ushering his sons into action.

Angus joined Davy in the kitchen area and they loaded the turkey, ham, and vegetables onto serving dishes and carried them to the table. When they returned to assemble the drinks and condiments, Angus peeked at their family to make sure they were occupied, then sauntered closer to Davy and murmured under his breath, "So, what's really going on with Evie? The truth, brother."

Davy looked upward as if considering how much to share. "The truth is…" He took a deep breath, then released it slowly. "Exactly what she said. There's nothing to know."

Angus chuckled. "You bastard. You really had me going."

"You should have known better, kid. What happened between us at school is ancient history. Let sleeping dogs lie."

"It's a pity," he replied. "She's a looker, and from what I remember, a real good sort, too."

"Forget it."

At the dining table, Mariko and Eileen laid out dinner plates, glasses, and cutlery while Hugh kept Reo busy with a toy tanker truck. Evelyn edged in, looking unsure of herself, and started chatting quietly to Hugh as he and the boy played.

"Lunch is ready," Davy announced, capturing everyone's attention. His family hastened to their seats, Mariko balancing her son on her knee. They left two chairs free, beside each other. One for Davy and one for Evelyn. Not subtle in the slightest. He met Evelyn's gaze and she gave him a wry smile, aware of the maneuver to force them together. She didn't seem surprised, either. Then again, she probably encountered this type of behavior all the time. Who wouldn't want a vibrant, vivacious woman to be part of their family, even if she were something of a loose unit?

She slid into the empty seat beside Eileen, glanced at the cutlery and hesitated, as if unsure of the proper protocol for a Christmas meal.

Davy came to her rescue. "Mam, would you like to say grace?"

Eileen pressed her palms together, bowed her head, and murmured, "Bless us, O Lord, and these, thy gifts, which we are about to receive from Thy bounty. Through Christ, our Lord. Amen."

Davy stole a look at Evelyn and noticed she'd bowed her head, too, muttering a furtive "Amen" afterward. He added his own voice to the chorus. "Amen. Dig in, everybody." He served himself a generous portion of everything. "Isn't this better than hiding out in the spare room?" he asked under his breath.

"I'm reserving judgment," she said. "Until after dessert."

"Good call."

"Evelyn," his mother said. "Tell me, what do you do?"

Davy thought the question may unsettle her, considering she was notoriously fickle when it came to employment, but she remained unruffled. "I'm between jobs at the moment. A friend in Timaru has offered me work at her orchard until I find something new."

"What kind of work are you looking for?" Hugh asked, splashing his turkey with sauce.

"I've worked in a wide range of fields. I have no qualifications, but I'll give almost anything a shot, and that seems to go a long way."

"Damned right, it does," Hugh agreed. "Too many young people these days are allergic to honest hard work. Would you like me to ask around? It's busy season on the farms, and one of my friends may need an extra worker."

"Thank you, that's very kind, but I might only be staying in the area temporarily. I'm not sure where I'm headed next."

Eileen frowned, and caught her husband's eye, her matchmaking temporarily thwarted. "Is Itirangi not home for you? I thought Angus said you grew up here."

Evelyn shoveled parsnip into her mouth, delaying her response. "I grew up here, but now I'm a nomad, really."

Eileen brightened again. "If you don't have roots elsewhere, why not take a job here for a while? Especially if there's a shortage of farmhands."

"Mam," Davy warned, concerned his houseguest would burst into tears again if pushed.

"No, it's all right." Evelyn flapped a hand in his direction. "The truth is, my mum passed away last year, and I have so many memories of her here that I'm not sure if I'm ready to be back yet."

Well that stopped his determined mother in her tracks. Because, really, how could anyone argue with grief? He felt a stab of admiration for Evelyn and her evasive tactics. The woman was cleverer than anyone gave her credit for. While it was true that her mum had died here last year, she'd wanted nothing to do with Itirangi for much longer than that.

Before the silence became awkward, she asked, "What was it like growing up in Ireland?"

And just like that, the conversation restarted. Davy stifled a laugh. She'd accidentally hit upon Eileen's favorite topic: the homeland.

∾

DAVY ROCKED his chair onto its rear legs, sighing with satisfaction. His belly was warm and full, he had his family around him, and it was Christmas. What could be better?

A sultry laugh sounded to his right. *Evelyn.* His family had taken to her, and watching her interact with them reminded him of a maestro conducting an orchestra. She ensured everyone was included in the conversation, redirected questions she didn't want to answer, and coaxed little Reo out of his shell until he demanded to sit on her lap rather than Mariko's.

She was in her element. Once she'd overcome her initial misgivings about intruding on their Christmas, she'd become the focal point of the dinner table, which was quite a feat considering she was the outsider.

In short, his family loved her. A fact that both gratified and terrified him. Once upon a time, he'd been nuts about her and had felt certain she'd fit in with his family, if only she'd give them a chance. It was nice to know he'd been right.

But.

Remember how that had ended? He'd fallen for her hard, and as soon as he'd started making plans for the future, she'd ditched him and never looked back. Sighing, he flicked a crumb from his lap, and as he moved, Reo grabbed his hand to study the digital watch around his wrist.

"Hey, buddy, let Uncle Davy eat," Evelyn said, gently dislodging him.

Davy caught his mum's eye across the table, and what he saw there spelled trouble. She'd been watching Evelyn with Reo as though she'd never seen anything like it.

"Do you have any nieces or nephews?" she asked.

"Nope," Evelyn replied. "I'm an only child."

"I'd never have guessed," Hugh said. "You seem so comfortable with Reo."

"I spent some time as a live-in nanny in Invercargill." She chuckled. "Talk about a steep learning curve. But I love kids, so it worked out great. I would have stayed in that position for longer, but the family moved to Australia and I didn't fancy making the move with them. I love Oz, but I wouldn't want to live there."

Her itchy feet had limits. Interesting.

Eileen had stars in her eyes. "I love children, too," she exclaimed. "I always wanted a whole bevy of grandkids. Reo is a good start, but I wouldn't mind another three or four to spoil. It's so nice to meet a young woman who likes children. They all seem to be focused on their careers these days."

"I see no reason why we can't have both," Evelyn said, earning Eileen's eternal devotion. Something bumped Davy's foot beneath the table. Glancing up, he saw Angus waggle his eyebrows.

"You must get lonely in this big, empty apartment all by yourself," Angus said, scratching his chin as though the thought had just occurred to him. "Surely it gets too quiet sometimes."

Uh-oh, he was in trouble now.

"I manage," he said through gritted teeth. The traitorous backstabber. "I like the peace and quiet. I see enough of people during the day. I need to recharge at night."

"Nonsense," Angus continued, ignoring the warning in his eyes. "You could have another five people here and hardly notice them."

"You could," Mariko agreed, not seeming to detect the undercurrent of the conversation. "It's such a large space for one person. I worry about you here by yourself. Why don't you get a roommate?"

"That's a nice idea," Davy said, "but I don't need a roommate. Trust me, I'm happy having the place to myself."

"He's telling the truth," Evelyn interjected. "If he had a roommate, he couldn't walk around in the nude. He forgot I was here this morning and wandered in, naked as the day he was born. I was doing yoga. He nearly frightened me out of my wits."

Silence met her statement. Then Eileen's lips twisted disapprovingly and Angus howled with laughter, slapping his thigh and hooting. "Oh, brother. That's too rich! What a way to dent a guy's ego. I hope you screamed."

"I don't think I did," she said thoughtfully. "But I can't remember for sure."

"You didn't." Davy's fists clenched in his lap hard enough that his nails bit into his palms. "I'd remember if you had." Shoving the chair back, he stood. "If you're all done laughing at my expense, I'm going to start cleaning up." Piling empty bowls on top of each other, he lugged them to the kitchen sink, stacked them inside, and ran some soapy water. His mother followed with the turkey and ham, and began packing leftovers into containers to store in the fridge.

"I like your Evelyn," she murmured, low enough not to be overheard. "She's delightful. You should hold onto her."

"She's not *my* Evelyn," he groaned, exasperated. "She's just passing through. We barely know each other anymore, and she's not even the tiniest bit interested in me."

She tilted her head and quirked a brow, clearly not believing him. "Take it from an old woman with years of wisdom, you could win that girl over if you really wanted to. I've been watching the two of you all night. You looking at her, her looking at you, both of you pretending not to. Don't dismiss it out of hand, that's all I'm asking. I can wait another few years for a grandbaby."

He nodded noncommittally. "I'll think about it."

But her offhand comment had intrigued him more than he cared to admit. Was Evelyn really interested in him? Despite the flare of attraction he'd seen earlier, he wouldn't have thought so. Now, he wondered. Damned if he didn't want to know.

———

8

While the O'Connors said their goodbyes, Evie snuck back to the spare bedroom and closed the door with a soft click. Stretching out on the bed, she rested her head on the pillow and closed her eyes.

Thank God for the quiet. She enjoyed being around people, but she'd been through the emotional equivalent of a spin cycle, and she was wrung out.

Davy knocked on the door.

Davy.

Another reason for the turbulent confusion turning her world topsy-turvy. She'd never have guessed his family would embrace her as they had—eager to welcome her into the fold. Or perhaps she'd secretly been afraid they would, making it even more difficult to leave. Perhaps that was why she'd really refused to meet them. She didn't know anymore.

"What is it?" she asked.

He peered around the corner and smiled, brackets forming around his mouth. "I'm heading down to the school for a friendly game of rugby with the boys. Are you up to joining me, or do you need a little time?"

"Ugh, I don't know." The idea of getting outside and

enjoying the sun appealed, but showing up to a social event with Davy would raise questions she didn't want raised, and what's more, she hadn't thrown a rugby ball in her life. Not that she'd admit as much to him. He'd been a member of the local team since primary school, and frankly, her inexperience was downright unpatriotic.

She'd watched games aplenty. A girl couldn't get by in New Zealand without watching the odd All Blacks game, especially if she frequented bars or worked in hospitality, but she'd moved around so much that joining a sports team had seemed like a waste of time. After a while, it simply became too embarrassing to admit she couldn't play. Better to pretend disinterest.

"There's not much I can do with that answer," he said. "Why don't you come along and you can lie in the sun if you don't want to take part?"

She supposed that sounded okay. "You've convinced me. Give me five minutes."

"How about two?"

She rolled her eyes. "Don't push your luck, Irishman." Just to be contrary, she took her time getting ready, changing into leggings and a soft jersey because the summer air was beginning to cool. She redid her mascara and added a layer of fiery red lipstick. A touch of body shimmer lotion on her cheekbones and cleavage, and she was done.

They drove to the sports field in Davy's station wagon, with Evie in the passenger seat. "So, who will be at this rugby game?" she asked.

"The usual suspects. Gareth, Justin, Cooper, Ramsay, Blake, Hemi, maybe a few others."

Evie winced. With Gareth, Cooper and Justin present, there were more than fifty-fifty odds her friends would find out she'd spent Christmas day with Davy—and also that she'd been in town and not let them know. Less than ideal. While she hadn't been in the mood to be with people until

Davy talked her around, she'd never want to hurt their feelings.

They arrived, and parked on the gravel area beside the field. Pine trees ringed the grass, with the exception of the side nearest to the makeshift parking lot and a small, weathered clubroom was to the right of the playing field. Evie caught sight of a woman with a mass of ginger hair standing with the group of men near the clubhouse. Her pulse flew into overdrive and she ducked behind the dashboard. *Emily.* Damn. Evie liked Emily—she was impossible to dislike—but if Emily was here with Justin, then the chances were that the other men had brought their girlfriends, too.

"If you wanted to be on your hands and knees, all you had to do was ask," Davy said, his tone laced with amusement.

She swatted his thigh. "This isn't funny. I thought you said it would just be the guys here."

"I thought it would be. Guess I got it wrong, sorry."

"I need to know whether Avery and Sophie are out there."

Davy scanned the group, who'd begun to turn their way.

"Yes, 'fraid so. Emily and Kayla, too."

Evie groaned. "Not good," she muttered to herself. "Not good at all." Then, more loudly, she said, "Can you take me back to your place?"

Davy stared at her as if she were insane. "No. We just got here. I'm sorry I didn't realize the girls were coming, but they're your friends, and I'm not just going to do a U-turn and leave. As soon as I do, they'll all ask why, and I'll be forced to explain how you spent all of last night in my arms and were too embarrassed to face them today."

She snorted. "You wouldn't."

He smirked. "Oh, I would."

Her lips twisted into a sneer. "You bastard."

He shrugged the insult off. "Been called worse. But I'd hate to tell my Mam you impugned her honor."

Impugned. What kind of pretentious dickhead actually used a word like that? And to think she'd been admiring his muscular forearms on the steering wheel only moments earlier.

"Don't worry about taking me all the way back," she said, prepared to bargain with him. "If you let me out at the school gate, I'll walk to your place."

"Evelyn, I'm not driving you anywhere."

Asshole. This could *not* be happening. She'd spent the night at his place specifically to avoid her friends—and yes, she knew how awful that sounded.

"I'll stay here," she said, in a last-ditch effort both to save face with her friends, and take away the risk of hurting their feelings.

Davy chuckled. "You can't hide on the floor of my car for the next few hours. Suck it up, buttercup. It will be okay. I promise."

"I suppose it'll have to be." She straightened, miming over-the-top movements to show anyone watching that she'd been searching for her earring on the floor, then fastened the imaginary earring in place and threw the door open without a backward glance.

"Hey, girls!" she cried, running toward her friends, arms outstretched.

Seeing her, Sophie leapt to her feet and met her halfway, yanking her into a fierce embrace. "Merry Christmas." She kissed Evie's cheek. "It's been way too long since I saw you. How come you're here?"

Evie shrugged, nonchalant. "You know me, always turning up like a bad penny. How have you been? How's that sexy man of yours?"

Sophie flushed scarlet and Evie knew she'd struck distraction-tactic gold. Sophie had been dating their friend Aria's older brother for a few months now, and though Evie had been surprised by the pairing at first, it made sense as soon as she saw them together. Their chemistry was hot as hell.

"He's fine as ever," Sophie said, her lips quirking up.

The truth in that smile kicked Evie in the heart. Sophie was happy. Really happy. After wasting years of her life on losers, she deserved it, but seeing the contentment that ran soul-deep hit a little close to home. Evie had never looked like that, not even close, and if she kept living the same nomadic lifestyle, keeping people at a distance, she doubted she ever would.

"Did he play Dirty Santa for you?" she teased, twirling a lock of Sophie's hair around her finger. "Don't tell me you haven't jumped his bones today; I can see it written all over you. You have that whole loved-up, post-orgasm look."

"Shh," Sophie hissed, her eyes darting to each side to check no one had heard. "There was no Dirty Santa role play, but we definitely celebrated Christmas the way it should be."

"Good girl."

"So, where'd you run into Davy?"

Evie pretended not to hear her, turning and waving at Avery, who was walking toward them.

"Fancy seeing you here." Avery hugged her. "I thought you were down south."

"I finished my job at the cafe two days ago," Evie explained. "I'm heading to Timaru to pick berries until I find another one." No need to mention her existential crisis.

Both women nodded.

"How'd you meet up with Davy?" Avery asked, eyes narrow above her aquiline nose.

Time to fib like a pro. "I hitched a ride from Oamaru to Itirangi. He saw me walking and suggested I come along to catch up with you guys."

From the way Avery's brows knitted together, Evie could tell her friend didn't believe her. Ever the scientist, she tended towards skepticism, while Sophie trusted people, often to her detriment.

Sophie smiled. "I'm glad you did. I haven't seen you since Lauren was born."

"Speaking of, how is the little bundle of joy?"

"She's adorable. Met her grandparents for the first time today, but that's not the biggest news of all. Ask Avery."

Evie turned to Avery expectantly. With a grin, Avery flashed her left hand and the sun glinted off a diamond on the fourth finger. A sparkling solitaire set in a white gold band.

Evie jumped on the spot, clapping her hands. "Oh my God! I'm so excited for you, girlfriend. When did it happen? How did he propose?" Gripping Avery's hand, she tugged it closer to study the ring. "He had to pick the biggest rock in the shop, didn't he?"

Avery chuckled, deep and throaty. "Slow down. One question at a time. He proposed just before lunch, at Aria's place. Nothing over the top, just handed me the ring and asked." She angled it until it dazzled the both of them. "It *is* gorgeous. He did well."

"Probably took Caro with him to help," Evie said, referring to Gareth's sister. "Have you set a date?"

"Slow down," she repeated. "We only got engaged a few hours ago. It'll take a while to sort out the details. It may surprise you, but I'm not one of those girls who planned their entire wedding when they were five."

"I'm shocked." Evie released her hand. "Shocked and appalled."

Avery snort-laughed. They both looked at Sophie, who flushed. While Avery had never been the marrying kind, Sophie had probably decided on a color scheme before she'd been old enough for high school. She'd had a romanticized view of marriage, seeing it as the ultimate security blanket, but these days she had a hottie of her own and didn't seem to be in such a rush to tie the knot.

"Merry Christmas, Evie."

Glancing up, she realized the others had joined them. Emily smiled, and hugged her. Out of the corner of her eye, she noticed Justin watching them. She nodded to him, and he jerked his chin in response. He wasn't exactly the chatty type, but he never let his girl out of his sight and Emily more than made up for his reserve with her bubbly personality.

"Merry Christmas, Em," Evie replied. "Hi, Kayla."

Where Emily was redheaded, curvy and gorgeous, her best friend Kayla was a petite blonde with glasses and straight-edged bangs.

"Hey, there," Kayla said. "Shall we find somewhere to sit? I think the guys are about to begin, and we want to make sure we're out of their way."

They made their way to the sideline, and Evie lay on her back, closing her eyes and basking in the remaining sunlight. Perhaps this wouldn't be so bad after all.

9

"Join us."

"Excuse me?" Evie used her hand to shield her face against the sun as she peered up at Gareth, who'd included all of the women in his invitation.

"We need more numbers," Davy, who'd accompanied him, said. "Would you ladies do us the honor of joining the game?"

"I'm in," Avery replied, taking Gareth's hand and letting him haul her upright.

"Me, too," Sophie said, leaping up.

Emily shook her head. "Sorry, boys, but I'm happy watching."

Kayla looped an arm around Emily's shoulders. "I'm with Em, but you guys have fun."

Davy raised an eyebrow at Evie. "You in?"

She wanted to. The weather was beautiful and the company was of the best variety, but she'd make a fool of herself. What kind of kiwi woman had never thrown a rugby ball?

"I'll keep these girls company," she said, gesturing at Kayla and Emily, ignoring the wistful part of her that wanted to be in on the fun.

"Really?" Davy asked. "I would've thought you'd want to be in the thick of it."

She pursed her lips. "Maybe you don't know me as well as you think you do."

Gareth's cheek muscles twitched. She got the impression he was trying not to laugh.

Davy shook his head. "If you can look me in the eyes and tell me you don't want to, I'll believe you."

She sighed, and tucked a strand of hair behind her ear. "I can't, but—"

"Then it's decided." He beamed. "You're playing, which means we have even teams of five."

With a look, Evie implored Avery and Sophie to rescue her, but Sophie was too busy ogling her boyfriend's admittedly great ass, and Avery just smirked. She probably thought this was karma or something.

Realizing no rescue was imminent, she beckoned Davy closer. He leaned down and she whispered in his ear, "I've never played before. I don't know how."

His brows shot toward his hairline, his expression becoming incredulous. "Never?" he asked softly. "Surely you've played a social game, or learned during PhysEd at school."

She glanced down. "The thing is, I might have skipped PhysEd once or twice." Or every class she'd ever had. She'd dropped it as soon as she was able, and before that she'd preferred making out with the stoners behind the gym to actually participating. She'd reasoned that knowing how to kick a ball would never get her anywhere, whereas Robbie with the long hair and dreamy eyes might have been the next Kurt Cobain.

"You naughty girl."

Her eyes met Davy's, his green gaze holding her captive. She wished she could fan herself, but as it was, nobody else seemed to have noticed the way he looked at her, and she didn't want to draw their attention to it.

"We both know I wasn't a goody-two-shoes," she said. "So anyway, I really can't play. You'd be better off being a player short. I'd just get in the way." She heard how self-pitying she sounded and hated it. In twenty-four hours, he'd seen all the worst of her, and now she felt two feet tall in his presence.

Davy tutted. "I never thought I'd see the day Evelyn Parata sounded sorry for herself. Where's your fighting spirit? Pull yourself together, toots. I'll give you a quick demo, and you can come on my team."

"I'll be a liability," she muttered.

"Don't take things so seriously. It's a social game amongst friends. We might shit-talk each other, but it's all in good fun. Come on, you know you want to."

She did want to. With a good-natured sigh, she agreed. "You're going to regret this."

"I seriously doubt that, sweetheart."

How Evelyn could have made it to the ripe old age of twenty-seven without having thrown a rugby ball was beyond Davy. Even Mariko had joined a game or two, and she was a pencil pusher who topped the scales at 90 pounds.

What surprised him more was how badly he wanted her to let loose on the field with him and the guys. She needed some fun, anyone could see that. He shouldn't care one way or the other—heck, if he were being honest, he should probably prefer for her to sit out and create some distance between them—but instead, here he was, standing so close to her he could feel the nervous energy vibrating through her compact little body.

"Hold the ball like this," he said, first showing her, then guiding her hands into the correct position. "You should have a hand at each end, with each of your thumbs on a seam, like this."

She made a decent attempt.

"Almost," he told her, "but keep your palms off the ball. Hold it with your fingers and thumbs."

"Like this?" she asked, adjusting her grip.

"Perfect." So what if the rest of her looked awkward as hell, the proud smile she gave him had his engine revving. *Cool your jets, boy.*

"How much do you know about the rules?" he asked.

"A little. I've watched a few games, just never played."

"So you know you can't pass forward?"

She nodded.

"Great start." He tugged the ball from her. "When you pass, turn your core to face the person you're passing to, and the right hand provides the power, the left hand just guides it. Like this." He demonstrated the passing motion, then tossed her the ball. "Your turn."

His stomach muscles tightened as he watched her blink rapidly, then close her eyes and draw in a long, even breath. She positioned her hands exactly as he'd shown, rotated her torso in a controlled movement, and threw the ball. It bounced along the ground and came to a stop when Hemi stepped on it.

"You've got it," he said, clapping her on the back. "Now all you need to remember is to run toward the opponent's end of the field and pass backward. Your teammates will take care of the rest. Think you can handle that?"

Her eyes were bright now, fear banished, and knowing he'd had a hand in that warmed him from the inside.

"I'm good to go, Captain." She bumped fists with him, then spun away and skipped across the field, trying to snatch the ball from Hemi, who resisted at first, then let her take it. As soon as her hands were full, he tickled her ribcage. She bent over, gasping for breath, the ball tucked tightly in her arms, refusing to surrender.

Even while his heart lifted to see her laugh after how she'd sobbed earlier in the day, Davy's throat went dry at the sight of her playfighting so comfortably with Hemi. He shoved his hands into his pockets.

It's none of your business who she flirts with.

Nevertheless, his rarely-beheld redheaded temper flared as he stalked over to the others. Had anything ever happened between Evelyn and Hemi? They made an attractive couple, and were equally outgoing. No doubt Hemi was the type to appeal to her, with his unflappable self-confidence, dark good looks and *Ta Moko* tattoos. He certainly appealed to most of the other women in town.

"We ready to go?" Gareth asked when Davy reached them.

A chorus of yeses rang out, with a couple of cheeky 'yes, Sergeants' thrown in.

Gareth continued, "On my team, I've got Justin, Hemi, Sophie and Blake. Davy, you've got Cooper, Ramsay, Avery and Evie. Split up."

The group divided in two as he'd ordered.

"Why didn't he choose Avery for his team?" Evelyn asked once they were out of earshot. "She's his fiancée, and super competitive."

Davy huffed a laugh, dipped his head, and murmured in her ear, "Gaz likes it when Avery gets fired up. If they're on different teams, he has a legitimate reason to tackle her."

Was it his imagination, or did she lean closer?

"Oh," she said, nodding in understanding. "Sneaky devil."

EVIE SHIVERED. She didn't know what strange chemical reaction was responsible, but each time Davy came near enough to touch, every muscle in her body quivered, and electric currents raced over her skin. She'd tried to ignore it during their impromptu ball-throwing lesson, but when he whispered in her ear, the sensation of his breath tickling her sensitive skin was too much, and her lips parted, a soft sigh escaping them.

Immediately, she clapped her mouth shut and pressed her lips into a firm line, eyes darting around to see if anyone had noticed. None of her team had, thank God, and though Davy watched her speculatively, he held his tongue for once in his life.

"Team huddle," he said, and they formed a tight circle. "Here's the plan."

Two minutes later, feeling slightly dazed, she had even less clue about what to do than she had before. She tried to recall what Davy had said earlier. Run forward, pass back, let everyone else take care of the rest. She could do that.

The teams lined up. She found an empty patch of grass and claimed it as her own, assuming a hunch-backed position, knees bent, hands in front of her with palms facing forward. She suspected she looked ridiculous, but it would hardly be the first time, and it wouldn't be the last. Someone whistled, and everyone leapt into action.

For the first few minutes, all she could do was run back and forth, just inside the sideline, slightly behind the person with the ball, in case they wanted to pass it. No one did. Then, only yards in front of her, Avery sprinted toward the opposing goalposts and Gareth lunged at her, grabbing her about the waist and knocking her to the ground. Avery dropped the ball and they both rolled to the side.

Before she'd even thought about doing anything, Evie had swooped in and grabbed the ball, squealing in surprise as Hemi tried to tackle it from her. She stumbled over her own feet, righted herself, and then she was flying across the field, exhilaration giving her wings. That was when she realized: nobody was going to catch her. She might be small, but she was speedy, and she'd had a good head start. Feet thundered in the background, gaining on her, but she'd nearly reached the end. She knew what to do. She'd seen dozens of All Blacks in this same position, even if she'd never dreamed she'd be here herself. Keeping low, she launched herself over the back line, touching the ball down as she skidded across the lush grass.

"Yes!" she cried, rising to her knees and whooping with excitement. "I did it!"

Sophie jogged to her side and high-fived her.

"Hey," Gareth yelled. "We don't congratulate the enemy."

Sophie rolled her eyes, and tugged Evie to her feet. "Nice work."

Avery slung an arm around her shoulders. "Go, you."

Davy held his hands out for the ball, and Evie threw it to him, pleased when it didn't veer too far off course.

"Not too shabby, newbie," he called. "Now the rest of you scram, so I can score us a conversion."

The girls hurried out of his way and Evie exchanged high-fives with Cooper and Ramsay as she rejoined her team. Play resumed, and she grinned until her cheeks ached, feeling lighter than she had in weeks.

10

When the game finished, they adjourned to Ramsay's bachelor pad, barely a block away, for drinks and a barbecue. While Ramsay and Hemi fired up the grill, Evie snagged a beer from the chiller and flopped onto one of the chairs on the lawn.

Glancing about, she was reminded that she was the only single lady here. On the deck, Avery bickered with Gareth, and Justin pressed Emily firmly to his side. Evie couldn't blame him—given half a chance, most of the single men in Itirangi would make a move on his girl. Heck, if Emily swung both ways, Evie would make a move on her. The redhead had more curves than an hourglass. Opposite Evie, Sophie perched on Cooper's lap, giggling at something he'd said. A few seats over, Kayla and Blake passed a bottle of beer back and forth.

Evie scrunched her nose. Gag. Too cute.

She contemplated the unattached men working the barbecue. Both Hemi and Ramsay were good-looking, in their own ways—Hemi dark and dangerous, Ramsay the kind of clean-cut man women introduced to their parents. She and

Hemi had always been great mates, and never wanted anything more than that. They were too similar. It'd be like sleeping with her brother. Ramsay, on the other hand, was too buttoned up for her taste. The local doctor seemed to think he could never let loose lest his clients hear about it and desert him in favor of the exactly *zero* other doctors in town.

Everyone was accounted for, except Davy.

"Enjoying the view?" an accented voice murmured near her ear. She turned to see Davy bent over the back of her chair, resting on his elbows above her, his nose only inches from hers.

"Always," she replied. "No better view than hot guys cooking. Well, unless they're wearing aprons, and nothing else."

"You witch." He chuckled. "Objectifying those poor men. I hope you're ashamed of yourself."

"Oh, I am." She shamelessly watched Ramsay's backside as he flipped steaks and fried onions. "So very ashamed."

"As you ought to be." Davy paused, and Evie met his mossy eyes. "You look relaxed."

"I suppose I am." Her misery from earlier that morning felt like it had been days ago, rather than hours. So much had happened since then.

"I'm pleased to hear that." He twinkled at her. "I can't abide the thought of you being so sad."

"Shh," she hissed, putting her finger to her lips despite the flutters stirred by his sweet words. "Don't talk like that. Someone might hear you."

"Aw, sweetheart. Are you embarrassed to be seen with me?" He smirked. "Hate to break it to you, but people are gonna wonder why we arrived together. This is Itirangi. You remember how the gossip vine works."

She groaned. "It's impossible to forget." She'd never succeeded at flying under the radar, though to be fair, she'd rarely tried. "By the way, I told them I was hitchhiking and you picked me up."

Coming around the chair, he sat beside her, and though they were well spaced, she felt crowded. "Good to know." He paused for a moment, then added, "I didn't think it bothered you," he said. "The attention, I mean. It doesn't seem to stop you from hooking up with a different guy every time you visit my bar."

He'd noticed?

Of course he had. It probably confirmed his opinion of her as a heartless she-devil.

But that didn't quite ring true. Not any longer. Perhaps he'd been jealous. *Don't go there, girl.* Even if he was, it would be best if she didn't dwell on it. That would only be one more way she'd hurt him.

"Tourists," she said, shrugging. "Never going to see them again, so what does it matter?"

She'd only made out with those guys to distract herself from Davy. Maybe that did make her heartless, but she couldn't handle the memories that arose when she was near him, or the knowledge that she was responsible for ending one of the best things she'd ever had.

She waited, expecting him to go on, but to her surprise, he stayed silent. Strange. With every conversation they had, she realized more and more that neither of them were the same people they had been. Time had taken the sharp edges off their moods.

Finally, he said, "You know, this is the first time we've really spoken in nine years. Why don't you tell me what you've been doing since we left school? You must have some great stories."

"Depends on what kind of stories you want to hear."

A smile flirted with the corner of his lips, and the glimpse of white teeth did funny things to her insides. "Dodging the question? Not your style."

She nodded toward the barbecue. "Bring me a sausage in bread, loaded with sauce and onions, and I'll tell you anything you want."

"Anything?"

The wicked gleam in his eye sent tingles racing down her spine, and her breath caught. She'd seen that expression before, usually seconds before he dragged her into his embrace and kissed her as if the universe depended on it. She needed to regain control of the situation, but she had never been good at resisting trouble when it came calling. Reaching across, she stroked a finger along the contour of the muscle in his forearm, which was lean and covered by freckly skin and rust-colored hair.

His fists clenched. Then he stood and pushed the chair back, his movements jerky. "I'll get you that sausage."

Both of them ignored the double entendre. Evie's head fell back and she gazed up at the stars that were only now beginning to appear, smiling smugly. She still had it. He still wanted her. Damn, but it felt good to be wanted by Davy.

A bread-encased sausage floated into her field of view, bringing with it the scent of sweet onion and mustard. She reached for it and sank her teeth into the crisp end, which tasted charred, and nearly seared her mouth. Sauce oozed from the side and dribbled down her chin. She hummed contentedly, wiping it up with a finger. Summer barbecues with beer, meat, music and friends. Nothing could beat that.

"Penny for your thoughts."

She blinked lazily, and Davy came into focus. She waved a hand around. "Just thinking how nice this is. I don't always slow down enough to appreciate life."

"Always on the go," he remarked. "I remember that from before."

Before. Back when the sight of this gangly boy loping across the grass, a lopsided grin in place, had made her dream about forever, even as she'd broken out in a cold sweat at the thought of never seeing the world beyond Itirangi. They'd had a summer romance, but it had meant more to her than that, and she knew it had meant more to him, too.

"Seems like you kept moving after we finished school," he said. "Is there anywhere you haven't lived?"

She thought for a moment as she finished her sausage. "The west coast of the North Island. I've passed through, but haven't lived there. I've spent time pretty much everywhere else."

"Even Stewart Island?" he asked, referring to the heavily forested island off the southernmost point of the country, which was home to only one small town.

"I did a summer there looking after the predator traps to protect native birds."

"Wow." He whistled. "You really have gotten around."

"Hey!" She slapped his upper arm, hard enough to sting, even though she knew he was teasing.

"I didn't mean it like that," he said with a laugh.

"Don't care how you meant it."

"Of course you do." He was right, his intention was all that mattered. "So tell me what kind of work you've been doing."

She recognized the olive branch for what it was and took it. "A bit of everything, really. I've bartended, waitressed, cleaned, manned a checkout, made coffee, driven a tour bus, picked fruit, worked in a factory, harvested crops, milked cows, worked in retail, dealt cards at a casino, looked after the books for a couple of companies, managed a workshop… Guess I'm a jack-of-all-trades."

Davy folded his arms over his chest and studied her, his expression inscrutable. "You farmed?"

"Is that so hard to believe?"

He tipped his bottle back and drank, taking his time to reply. "A little bit. Milking isn't the most glamorous gig."

"I'm not the most glamorous girl."

He snorted. "I find that hard to believe. Every time I see you, you're dressed to kill."

"Davy, think," she said slowly, meaningfully. "Every time you see me, I'm at your bar. Of course I look my best when I'm out on the town. That's not me all the time."

He frowned as though this thought had never occurred to him.

"Most of the time, I'm frazzled and sweaty and less than my best. So yeah, I've worn overalls and been pissed on by a bunch of smelly cows, and I've been coated in dust at the end of a long day on a harvester, reeking of rotten potatoes."

He shook his head and held up a hand. "Stop talking, or I'll have to re-evaluate my opinion of you. I'm not ready for that much self-reflection."

Her lips twisted into a reluctant smile. "If it helps confirm your worst suspicions, I also danced at a topless club."

"You did *what*?" he demanded, rocking back into his chair, mouth gaping.

"I danced at a club," she said, shrugging. "Made good money. No biggie. Decided it wasn't for me. Most of the guys were fine, but there were a couple of creepers. The girls were lovely, though. I miss them a little." People as accepting as those dancers were few and far between. It was a pity that others weren't as accepting of them.

"Are you saying you were a stripper?" He looked ready to bust a vein in his forehead.

"Oh, for goodness sake, don't be stupid about it," she snapped. "It was something I tried. It's not like I was ever fully naked on stage, and nobody laid a finger on me. I'll tell you though, there are some places glitter just shouldn't go."

Color rose on his cheeks, and he wheezed a little. "I'm not bothered by it, but that *image*."

Edging closer, wearing a mischievous smile, she asked, "Why are you so red?"

He swallowed, his Adam's apple bobbing. "I know that you know the effect you have on me." His voice was hoarse. "And now I'm picturing you naked and covered in glitter. Have a little mercy, woman."

Watching him battle his attraction to her stoked something in Evie. She didn't want him to put that fire out, she wanted him to consume her with it. Though it might be the stupidest idea she'd ever had, she wanted to be with him, even if only for a while. She didn't know where she was headed after Monica's orchard, or what she even wanted out of the next year of her life, but today she'd felt more alive than she had in a long time, and that was thanks to him.

"What say we call it a night?" she asked after only a moment's hesitation. Maybe she'd regret this, maybe she wouldn't, but she made it her philosophy not to hold back from something she might enjoy because of fear. "You and me, head back to your place. Together."

Davy stared at her intently, like he was trying to read her soul. Then he croaked, "Hell, yes."

11

*D*avy and Evelyn barely made it inside his bar before falling into each other's arms. He kicked the door shut, swept her off her feet and deposited her on the counter. She parted her thighs and he stepped between them, turning his face up to her. His heart thumped wildly, pumping fire through his veins, his dick already hard. Evelyn's big brown eyes locked on his, and he could read the desire in them.

He couldn't believe this was happening. He was getting a do-over with this sexy goddess. She could have any guy she wanted with a crook of her finger, but she was here with him. He was under no illusion that they'd have anything more than one night together, but if that was all she could give, he'd take it. Hell, if she asked, he'd probably offer up his heart for her to stomp on all over again.

One of his arms curved around her waist, and the other hand cupped the line of her jaw. He hovered, mere millimeters from her mouth, feeling as though he were suspended above a thousand-foot drop. As though everything depended on what he did next. The anticipation of the kiss, the tortured bliss of waiting while they exchanged breath, almost did his head in.

But then their lips were touching. He hadn't kissed her, so she'd kissed him.

It was perfect.

Their lips clung, then separated, and the breath eased from his chest. She gripped his face between her palms and shimmied to the edge of the counter so they touched in all the best places.

This time, he took the initiative. He kissed her the way he remembered she liked, soft and unhurried. Her lips parted for him, and the kiss deepened. He clasped her tighter, one hand splayed over her hip and the other on her ass. She tasted like summer, and the forbidden, and he couldn't get enough.

Pulling back, he panted, "You sure?"

"One hundred per cent," she said, nuzzling beneath his ear, then touching his ear lobe with the tip of her tongue. "But…"

"But?" he croaked, keeping a tenuous hold of his self-control.

"But I want you to know, this means—"

"I know what it means," he interrupted. Nothing, at least as far as she was concerned, and he wasn't about to humiliate himself by begging for scraps of her affection "Don't suppose you've got a condom on you?"

She shook her head.

"Damn. Guess we'll have to drag ourselves upstairs."

Evie was short of breath as she ascended the stairs to Davy's home and waited while he unlocked the door. She couldn't believe how much he'd leveled up in the kissing game since they were sixteen. He was blowing her mind. Once inside, she pressed him into the door and leapt up, wrapping her legs around his waist. Behind his sports shorts, his cock pulsed against her.

She grinned as an answering throb started between her legs. "Someone's a little excited."

"Have to be dead not to be," he said. "You're the sexiest woman I've ever touched, and shite, the way you rub yourself against me drives me insane."

That's how she wanted it. As long as they were together in the insanity, all was right with the world.

Davy's forehead rested on hers, his chest rising and falling rapidly, the lines of his face made harsh by passion. She loved to see him this way. All need. No sign of his joker persona. She fused her mouth to his, tearing a low groan from him.

Fuck, yeah, she loved the sound of that. Like he was helpless, enraptured by her. Tugging the hem of his shirt, she broke away to yank it over his head, then tossed her own aside, too.

They slid against each other, skin on skin. Exquisite. She ran her hands along the tops of his broad shoulders and down his arms, which were tan in contrast to the paleness of his chest and shoulders. He buried his face in her exposed cleavage, his tongue delving into the space between, then tracing the edge of her bra. Pleasure shot through her as his hand came up to cup her breast. He dropped an open-mouthed kiss on the top and moaned in appreciation.

"These are perfect," he said. "God, I didn't think you could get any sexier, but you did. Take the bra off."

"Patience," she teased, her heels digging into his butt. His hips jerked towards her. "Oh yeah, just like that."

"You're gonna be the end of me," he murmured. "Death by heart failure, age twenty-eight."

"You poor baby." She pouted. "You're seducing me with your words." Strangely enough, he actually was. Most men adored her body—she was used to it—but his particular brand of humor flattered her more than any pretty words could.

"Hold tight, sweetheart," he said, then he was carrying her to the living room, where he lowered her gently to the couch and settled between her legs. The room was dim, but they'd forgotten to switch off the Christmas lights earlier and dozens of stars twinkled around them, casting pinpricks of light and shadows that danced over their bodies.

Reaching behind her, Evie flicked the clasp of her bra open and dropped it to the floor. Davy's gaze homed in on her naked breasts, then he molded his palms to them and stroked and caressed with a single-mindedness she found astoundingly attractive. The whole time, his eyes never left hers. He watched her watching him, interpreting what she liked and what she didn't from the play of expressions across her face. It was the single most erotic act she'd ever been involved in.

Damn, boy.

When she was desperate for more, she writhed beneath him, creating sweet friction between their bodies, and slipped one hand into the waistband of his shorts, wrapping her fingers around him.

"Mmm." He pumped his hips, thrusting into her hand.

"I love the sounds you make." She slicked the moisture at his head over the silken length and glided up and down. "Don't stop making those sounds."

He uttered a strangled gasp. "Don't think I could if I wanted. Feels goddamn fantastic."

"Good," she muttered. "I want you bad."

Rising on one elbow, he drew her leggings and underwear down and touched her gently. "Are you ready for me?"

"Check for yourself."

His finger slid between her folds, and when he discovered

how wet she was, his eyes flicked to hers. "Oh, hell. You do want me bad, don't you, sweetheart?"

"Like I said, so get a move on."

"Patience." He sheathed himself, then eased his tip inside her in increments, rocking forward an inch at a time.

"Davy," she growled in warning.

In one smooth movement, he pushed all the way home, lodging deep inside her with a satisfied grunt.

Breath hissed between her lips. *"Fuck."*

Davy froze. "Good or bad?" he asked. "Do I need to stop?"

"Good," she said. "Don't you dare stop or I'll kick your ass."

She heard him exhale in relief, but then she was too absorbed by the way he moved to notice anything else. She drew one of her knees up, opening herself to him, and he took advantage of the movement to thrust even deeper with long, steady strokes that had her whimpering and clutching his back.

Turning her face into his, she latched onto his lips and kissed him like it was the last time she'd ever taste a man. He groaned again, and the sound of sex filled the air. Wet slapping, panting, thumping. The noises he made had her hotter than she'd ever been, and the wilder she got, the more he moaned and grunted and sighed. She'd never craved release so desperately while also wanting a moment to go on and on and on.

Davy raised himself up, and she looked down at the place where the two of them joined, him sliding into her and withdrawing, then slamming back in again. His pale hips met her bronzed stomach, the contrast delicious.

"Oh, god," she gasped, overwhelmed by the sight.

"So hot." He dipped his head to suck her nipple.

She came with a violent shudder, the orgasm washing over her in waves, the intensity easing, then returning with a vengeance until all she could do was hold onto his shoulders and wonder if she'd ever feel so complete again in her life. His hands tucked beneath her body and lifted her to him. He pushed into her one more time and shouted her name as he jerked and twitched inside her. They collapsed in a blissful tangle of limbs.

"**E**velyn?"

Evie buried her face in the pillow and pretended not to hear him. The whole night had been wonderful. It had felt like the beginning of something life-changing, but they'd yet to talk about what it meant, except for that single aborted conversation, and she wasn't sure if she was mentally fortified enough to open the topic. What if he didn't view things the same way she did? She'd hurt him once before, so it would be reasonable for him to be a little reluctant to jump into something with her.

"Evelyn, darlin', you've got to wake up. The mechanic is here."

What?

She must have spoken out loud, because he repeated, "I said the mechanic is here."

She rolled over and sat up, blinking until her vision cleared, trying to make sense of his words. While she'd intended to call the mechanic, she never had. "What's he doing here?"

"I called him for you. I knew you'd be eager to hit the road again."

Touching a finger to her ear, she wondered if it had begun translating English incorrectly. Had she done something to give him the impression she wouldn't want to hang around and talk this through—or at the very least, eat breakfast and go for another round?

Her stomach roiled as a dreadful possibility occurred to her. Was he trying to get rid of her? Was this his way of letting her down gently? Disappointment stabbed through her, leaving a cold, aching hole in her chest. She rubbed it absently.

"Okay, I'll dress. Just give me a moment."

His ginger brows drew together and lowered over his deep green eyes. "I thought you'd be pleased."

"I am." Her tone was so flat she couldn't even fool herself. "Thank you, Davy, for helping me get on my way."

She sounded like a bitch, but she couldn't help it. She didn't want him to rush her out the door. She wanted him to make bagels and eat them in bed with her. For once in her goddamned life, she wanted to stay. But she wouldn't stay where she wasn't wanted. Her mama raised her to have more self-respect than that.

"I'd say 'you're welcome', but I'm not sure you really mean it. Where's your head at, Evelyn?"

She shook the aforementioned head. "Nowhere. Don't worry, I'm being silly." Come to think of it, being silly would have been expecting affection from her ex, years after she broke his heart and left him in her dust. Just because her priorities had changed didn't mean his feelings toward her had.

"Are you okay?"

No, but she would be. "Yeah, of course."

She climbed out of his bed, the cool morning air gliding over her naked body, and noticed his pupils dilate as he looked at her. He might not want her to stay, but he still *wanted* her, and that was something. She padded across the carpet to collect her clothes, and tugged them on under his watchful gaze. Then she brushed past him and went to the spare room, grabbed her toothbrush and deodorant, and headed to the bathroom to clean up.

Once she didn't stink and her breath tasted minty fresh, she zipped her suitcase shut and wheeled it out. Two minutes later, she was standing on the footpath outside the bar, where a stocky blond guy with a short beard was waiting.

"I'm Evie," she said, determined to smother her internal bitch because this guy was out here at the crack of dawn on Boxing Day and didn't deserve her snark. "Nice to meet you."

"Joe," he replied, shaking her hand with his own. His sleeves were rolled up to his elbows, revealing tattooed forearms. He was an attractive guy, and based on the way he scanned her, pausing at her butt and chest, she'd say he thought the same of her, but unfortunately, she felt no interest. Not so much as a flicker. All of her interest was reserved for the lanky redhead standing behind her, trying to usher her out of his life.

"I've already got your car rigged up," Joe said. "You good to go? Davy said you'd want to ride down with me and wait while I take a look under the hood."

"Oh he did, did he?" She tried to reign it in, reminding herself none of this was Joe's fault.

"Uh, yeah." He frowned. "So you coming, or what?" He tapped the side panel of his cab and gestured for her to get in.

"Guess so." She turned to Davy, wishing her heart didn't flip-flop like a traitor at the sight of his stupidly handsome face. "Thanks for everything." The words felt wholly inadequate after the time they'd passed together, but his expression didn't welcome anything more personal. "I'll see you round?"

He nodded. "Don't be a stranger." Then he ducked his head, pecked her lips, and stepped back a couple of paces.

Evie strode to the front of the cab, yanked the door open and leapt inside the scuffed leather interior. Then she lowered the window and waved, pretending a light-heartedness she didn't know if she'd ever feel again. "Merry Christmas, O'Connor."

"*Meri Kirihimete*, Evelyn."

She let out a slow breath, wound up the window, and smiled at Joe. "Thanks. I appreciate your help."

"No worries, honey."

DAVY RETURNED INSIDE, cursing himself for being an idiot—not an unfamiliar occurrence for him, especially when Evelyn was around. He drew the curtains back and watched the tow truck vanish around the corner, out of sight.

It had been the right thing to do, hadn't it?

He'd been more convinced before he saw the shock in her eyes, and the stiffness creeping into her body. When the smile on her plump lips had compressed itself into nonexistence, he'd had the horrid thought he may have misjudged things. But she hadn't said anything, just gone quiet and gathered her things. She hadn't yelled at him, as she used to when he was being a moron, and she hadn't tried to persuade him to rejoin her in bed. But then, she hadn't thanked him, either.

He sighed. He was overthinking this. They'd gotten caught up in the spirit of the holidays, nothing more. And yeah, he'd been happier in the brief time he'd spent with her than he had in months, but that didn't mean she felt the same way, and it certainly didn't mean anything would come of it. As far as he knew, nothing had changed. His life was in Itirangi, and hers was in whatever distant horizon she set her compass for next.

He cared for her, but so what? His wishing for her to love him didn't make it so.

He struggled for control of his emotions, but it was futile. He'd have to visit the gym and lift weights until his body was so weary he couldn't think of anything, but he wasn't sure even that would erase her from his mind.

As it happened, Evie's shitty car was unfixable, so she left it with the mechanic to use for parts, receiving a small payout in exchange—enough to get her through a couple of weeks at least. As the new year approached, she found herself bunking at her friend Monica's place near Timaru while she worked mornings and early afternoons picking berries. Everything was back to normal. She should be happy, but instead the discontent that had been simmering inside her for months had grown into a festering wound she couldn't ignore, much as she tried. And she *tried*.

She searched maps for her new destination, somewhere fun she could be excited about, but nowhere she considered brought more than a passing interest. Instead, she kept dwelling on Davy O'Connor, and his soulful eyes and hot body, and all the things she should have said to him rather than up and leaving as per usual.

She should have told him what Christmas had meant to her, what *he* meant to her, and asked for a second chance. Should have sent the mechanic away and seduced the reluctance right out of him. Hell, anything would have been better than just waving to him in the rearview mirror like she didn't give a shit about him. For the *second* time. He'd never want to see her again after this, and she couldn't blame him.

"Are you moping again?" Monica asked, coming into the living room, where Evie was curled on the couch with Monica's pug, Norman.

"Nah, I'm just giving Norm some love."

"Come on, babe." Monica folded her athletic frame into an armchair and ran a hand through her short, dark hair. "If you miss him that much, just call him."

Evie buried her face in Norman's soft fur and when she spoke, her voice was muffled. "It's not that simple." Nothing was simple when it came to her and the sexy Irishman.

"Sure seems it from here." Monica lounged back, stretching her legs out and resting her feet on the arm of the couch. "You like him, and he must like you, otherwise he wouldn't have gone on a trip down memory lane considering how you crushed him the first time around—"

"Hey!" Evie protested.

"—so just suck up your pride and tell him how you feel."

She groaned. "It sounds easy when you say it."

Monica's expression softened. "Not easy, babe, but not impossible, either. You're a full-steam-ahead kind of woman. Why are you being so cautious now?"

Evie honestly wished she knew. She'd thought it over a hundred times, but never gotten a useful answer. The truth was, perhaps she cared about this more than anything else she'd done. In the past, she hadn't been concerned about picking up her entire life and starting over, and over, and *over*, because the stakes hadn't been high. Sure, if things went south, she'd be stretched for cash for a couple of weeks, but she always landed on her feet.

When it came to building a relationship and putting down roots, the stakes were infinitely higher, and she wasn't sure she had the tools to succeed.

"I'll think about calling him," she conceded.

Monica raised an eyebrow, and Evie crinkled her nose in response. Yeah, she wasn't buying her bullshit either.

On New Year's Eve, Davy didn't want to celebrate anything. Unfortunately, it was one of his busiest days of the year. When his phone rang, he answered without checking caller ID.

"You've reached Davy of Davy's. What can I do you for?"

"Davy?" The voice belonged to a woman, and rose at the end in question. "This is Monica Jackman. Have you got a moment?"

"Not really, no." As it was, he was pouring a pint of beer with the phone pressed between his ear and his shoulder.

"It's about Evie."

Everything inside him froze. He hadn't heard that name out loud in days, although it had been on replay inside his head. "What about her? Is she okay?"

If something had happened to her before he'd had the chance to tell her how he felt, he'd never forgive himself.

"She's fine."

Of course she was. He relaxed, and pushed the beer over the counter, gesturing to his employees that he'd be back in a moment, then he headed into the stairwell, away from the noise of the bar. "Look, Monica, I run a bar and we're insanely busy right now so can you make it quick? What's this about?"

"She misses you."

His eyes bulged. "I beg your pardon?"

"She's staying with me, and she's been miserable ever since she arrived. I knew she wouldn't reach out to you on her own, although God knows why, so I thought I'd do it for her. Can the two of you please just talk to each other?"

"Erm." He swallowed. Hard. "What makes you think she misses me?"

Monica sighed, and even through the phone he could sense her eye-roll. "She talks about you every second sentence, she only gets out of her pajamas to work, and she's not her usual self."

Someone called his name, and he winced. The timing of this couldn't be worse. "I've got to—"

"Go," she finished for him. "I know. But promise me you'll talk to her." She paused. "She really cares about you."

"I will," he said, but she was gone. His heart hammered and he rested his forehead against the wall, willing it to calm down enough for him to go and serve the masses.

Evelyn missed him. Was it really possible? He bloody well hoped so, because some of the color had leached from his life when she left, and he found he didn't care about keeping his heart safe anymore—he wanted her back. If what Monica said was true, he'd do whatever it took to hold onto her, because he'd gone and fallen for her again. Every flighty, nutty, brilliant part of her. If that made him off his rocker, worse things had happened.

But before he could woo his lady, he had to make it through the night.

Kneeling amongst the raspberry bushes, Evie picked juicy berries from the branches and dropped them into a plastic punnet. The juice stained her fingers red, and her knees were dusty from the ground. When the punnet was full, she grabbed another and shuffled along to an untouched bush.

The sun had risen overhead, and it warmed her back pleasantly, not yet holding the true heat of a summer day. Birds and cicadas chirped, and in the distance, she could hear the music one of the other workers was playing on a Bluetooth speaker. The scent of nature, ripe fruit, and sunscreen swirled through the corridor between the rows of bushes, carried on the breeze. Her lips tugged up at the corners. While she could happily sleep a day away, she also loved being up and outside in the morning, and what better way to bring in a new year than by being out in nature?

Someone sneezed, and she wrinkled her nose in sympathy. A few of the others suffered from nasty bouts of hayfever. Thankfully, she didn't have that problem.

"Evie!"

She stood, stretched, and smiled at Monica. "Hey, Mon. What's up?"

Monica nodded in greeting and said, "Take a break. You've been at it for hours. The berries will still be here in ten minutes."

Evie grinned. "Not if someone else picks them first."

Monica's hands went to her hips. "Don't you sass me, girl. I'm your boss, remember."

Evie stacked her punnets into a crate. "I'm fine, Mon. Really. I could do this all day."

"That may be, but as your boss, I'm putting my foot down. Go get a drink, and lie down for a bit."

Evie didn't argue again, just nodded and watched Monica stroll off to boss someone else around. A break couldn't hurt —she'd been picking for the better part of five hours. One of the benefits of living with the boss was that she could start as early as she pleased.

Heading to the tap to refill her water bottle, she paused beside her backpack and wiped sweat from her forehead with a towel, then exited the fenced portion of the orchard and rounded the corner, coming to an abrupt halt before she reached her destination.

There, sitting cross-legged on a checkered red and white blanket with a picnic basket at his side, a few yards from the water tap, was Davy. Her heart stuttered at the sight of him. She hadn't expected to see him again until the next time the girls dragged her to his bar, and when that happened, she'd expected them to behave like polite strangers.

But now he was here. At her work. A million questions flew through her mind.

What was he doing here?

Was he here for her? And if so, why?

Had he always looked so damned *fine*?

In front of him lay an oval platter of finger foods. Cheese, crackers, fruit, chocolates. A bottle of wine rested against his knee, two paper cups beside it.

An actual, honest to god, picnic.

He grinned at her, and Evie felt an answering smile creep over her face.

"Morning, sweetheart," he said. "Happy new year."

"*Morena*," she replied, gesturing at the blanket. "What's all this?"

~

DAVY HAD NEVER SWEATED SO MUCH in his life. It trickled down the side of his neck, soaked the top of his shirt and dribbled down his spine, pooling above the waistband of his shorts. The morning was warm, but the primary reason for his excessive sweating was nerves. It had been days since he'd seen Evelyn, and now he'd turned up at her workplace unexpectedly. Worse, he'd conspired with her boss to get her here, working on the premise that she returned his feelings. But what if he was wrong? What if Monica had misread the situation?

When she'd first come into view, wearing tiny pink shorts with her hair tied back in a ponytail, a red bandanna wrapped around her head and her face free of makeup, he felt like he'd been struck over the head by a frying pan.

This is her.

The woman he wanted to spend years of his life getting to know. The one he wanted to see across the dinner table at family Christmases from now on. He was batshit crazy for her.

His mouth went dry as he took in every glorious inch of her, as if seeing her properly for the first time. And perhaps he was. The woman before him was someone who enjoyed travelling, but wasn't flaky. A hard worker, not afraid to learn new things. Most of all, she was someone who loved fun but had experienced life's ups and downs, too.

She took his breath away.

She'd never looked more beautiful.

He smiled. She smiled. They greeted each other.

His breathing quickened and his stomach knotted as he patted the blanket and said, "Will you join me?"

She hesitated, gnawing on her lip. "I have to go back to work soon."

"I spoke to Monica. She doesn't mind if you take fifteen minutes off to sit with me, but it's your choice."

After what seemed an eternity, she nodded. "Okay."

He went weak with relief. He'd gotten over one hurdle. Hopefully fifteen minutes was all he'd need to get over another. With shaky hands, he poured wine into one of the paper cups and handed it to her. She sipped, and watched him over the rim.

"Have something to eat," he said, and she selected a cracker and wedge of creamy cheese. He didn't touch the food. He was too nervous to eat, and he feared if he poured himself a drink, he'd spill it in his lap.

"This is nice," she said, waving the cracker.

He didn't know whether she was referring to the food or the setup, but either way, he'd take the compliment. "I'm glad you approve."

"What I can't figure out is what you're doing here."

Time to get to the point. As his dad would say, shit or get off the pot. "I want to be with you. I want to give 'us' a shot."

She stared at him like he'd sprouted a second head, the food and wine forgotten.

"I want to take you out, buy you dinner, go to the movies. Treat you right." When she still seemed utterly baffled, he asked, "Am I bungling this?"

"No," she said softly, shaking her head from side to side. "But I'm not sure exactly what you're saying."

He needed to put this simply. "I want to go on a date with you, sweetheart—a proper date—with no expectation of anything coming from it other than that we enjoy ourselves."

She cocked her head. "You're asking me on a date?"

"Yes." He grinned, his confidence growing since she hadn't run screaming or immediately rebuffed him. "My family would think I was crazy if I didn't. Do you know how many times they told me not to let you go? A lot."

Her mouth formed an "o" of surprise. "Ha! That's brilliant."

"You're brilliant."

She snorted. "Cheesy, O'Connor. Real cheesy."

"I know." He took the cup from her, balanced it on the ground, and held her hand in his own, ready to offer her his heart and pray she didn't break it again. "So, what I'm asking is, will you let me take you out? Will you wait just a while before you move away so we can see if we could have something real?"

Evelyn pondered it. Her brows lowered in thought. For every second she remained silent, his tension ratcheted up a notch. Finally, she pursed her lips and said, in the same casual tone with which she'd agreed to join him, "Okay, sounds like a plan."

"Yes?" he asked. "Just like that?"

A cheeky smile stretched across her face. "Did you want me to play hard to get?"

"Well, no." He floundered. "Frankly, I didn't know what to expect, but I didn't think you'd agree to stay so easily."

She laughed, and it lit her whole face. Her deep brown eyes glowed with affection. "Here's the thing, Irishman. I've been feeling a bit off for a while, and I haven't been able to figure out why, but I think I finally know. I'm tired of always being on the move." She shrugged. "I'm getting older, and there aren't many places I haven't seen. I'm ready to try something new. Something like staying."

"Seriously?" He came onto his knees and leaned over her, dropping a kiss on her lips. "You couldn't have said this a little earlier? Like, say, before we did the deed?"

Her smile turned wry. "You didn't give me the chance, and besides, I was still working it out for myself. You know me—I have to come around to things in my own time."

He kissed her again, because it was that or wring her infuriating neck. "Do you have any idea how crazy you make me?"

She grinned. "I think I need another kiss to remind me."

He obliged, and this time it was slow and all-consuming. He put every ounce of his feelings for her into it, hoping she could tell how serious he was. They drew back and he kissed her nose. Her eyes fluttered closed, and he kissed her eyelids. She giggled, her smile broadening.

"Work with me," Davy said impulsively. "Come and do my books. Help me in the bar. I'll need another staff member in the new year." A wonderful, crazy idea occurred to him. "Move in with me."

She burst out laughing, the sound light and happy and perfect. "Slow down, Irishman. One step at a time."

"Why?" he demanded, gathering her into his arms for a kiss. "There's plenty of space in my apartment for two."

She cupped his face between her palms. "That's not taking it slow," she said, her smile saying she didn't mind. She kissed his forehead. "Yes, I'll work with you. But you're not my boss. We don't need that clouding our relationship. I'll work with you as a private contractor. No, I won't live with you, but I will date you, and maybe one day we'll get there. We're not rushing anything. I want to be wooed."

He chuckled. What had he ever done to deserve this woman?

The sun reflected in her eyes and they seemed to twinkle. Her cupid's bow deepened, as did her smile. She was so beautiful.

"Have I told you I adore you?" he asked.

"No, but I wouldn't mind hearing that."

"I adore you." His hands steady, he helped himself to a cup of wine, then shifted to sit by her side, his arm around her shoulders. "Shall we have a toast?"

She snuggled into his side. "I propose a toast to you, Davy O'Connor. And to summer. And a brilliant start to a new year."

They clinked their paper glasses. "Cheers."

Then they stretched out on the blanket beneath the high morning sun and talked for far longer than fifteen minutes, but neither of them cared. All they cared about was getting to know each other again. Davy's heart was full and he'd never experienced such a wonderful moment as his second first date with Evelyn Parata.

The first of many.

THE END

MIDNIGHT KISSES EXCERPT

Take that, Chloe Somers.

Emily Parker shook her fall of long red hair out of the way and scrutinized the bridal bouquet—an arrangement of white orchids and roses. Satisfied, she placed it in the center of the wedding party's table She tweaked a single flower that had drooped, and adjusted the ribbon holding the bouquet together. *Perfect.* No one could possibly accuse her of doing a sub-par job just because she loathed the bride, not when she'd pulled together a masterpiece with hardly any notice. Moving on from the bridal bouquet, she set out four smaller bouquets in front of the seats marked for the bridesmaids and groomsmen. She eyed them critically.

Everything had to be just right.

Even though she would prefer not to be involved with this wedding—the second Chloe Somers wedding she'd been hired to decorate—she couldn't afford to turn down work. Not in a town the size of Itirangi, despite it becoming something of a wedding destination. Another year or two and she had no doubt her floristry business would be booming just like her gift store and commercial rental business. Happy couples were drawn to Itirangi by the gorgeous backdrop—

the azure lake that was glacier-fed and the stunning green-brown of the surrounding mountains and forests. The picture-perfect New Zealand town.

Over the past few weeks, foreigners and out-of-towners had descended upon the town in droves for their summer vacations, so Emily's gift shop was bustling, and all of her tenants in the refurbished heritage building she owned—ranging from book stores to artist studios to beauty parlors—were experiencing the same wave of activity. She could barely afford the time away to decorate the vineyard restaurant for Chloe's wedding.

At the thought of Chloe's previous wedding, Emily's stomach lurched uncomfortably. Planned for a little less than a year ago, that first wedding had been canceled two weeks before the big day, when Chloe had dumped the groom to run off with his second cousin—who, incidentally, was the groom of *this* wedding. Emily wanted to drag both Chloe and her fiancé over a field of hot coals.

But that didn't matter. What mattered was that this wedding actually *happen*. Though Emily would be paid either way, she could think of no better punishment for the groom, Rich Belvedere, who'd stolen another man's woman, than to live the rest of his days with Satan's Mistress as his wife. Furthermore, Emily was a professional, and firmly believed that everyone should have a beautiful wedding. She could put her feelings aside for as long as it took to give Chloe her dream wedding, and cash the paycheck.

Strolling outside to her car, Emily took a moment to enjoy the chirping of birds in the trees that ringed the graveled parking lot. The warm wind rustled through the vineyard behind her, carrying with it the scent of leaves and fruit. Sweat beaded on her forehead and she wiped it with the back of a hand. From her car, she retrieved an awkwardly-sized box where she'd stored the table centerpieces and maneuvered it back inside the restaurant, the weight causing her no problems because her arms were toned, accustomed to the heavy lifting.

Hands on hips, she surveyed the reception room, taking stock of the raw materials. A number of long rectangular tables covered by white tablecloths dominated the space, contrasting pleasantly with the wooden walls and floors. The large windows provided a beautiful view out over the vineyard. The place had good bones.

She started assembling the table decorations, an elegant arrangement consisting of silver candlesticks with towering white candles and simple but elegant bouquets. The candlesticks were heavy. She couldn't help but think she wouldn't mind whacking the bride upside her head with one. Gently, of course. Just enough to give her a shock. Payback for running out on a good man, and for the years of torment Emily had endured at her hands in high school.

Carrot top, Chloe had called her. *Chubby cheeks. Ginny Weasley.*

Actually, Emily hadn't minded the last one. But regardless, after being bullied by the gorgeous Queen Bee, she could barely stand to be employed by her. The past few days, Emily had needed every ounce of her patience, and regular sessions watching kitten videos on YouTube, to make it through.

"Hey, Em."

Emily swung around, her smile wavering at the sight of Justin Simons. His broad frame filled the doorway, and his thumbs were hooked into the pockets of his jeans. He looked crazy-handsome despite the faded clothes, the halo of unruly dark hair, and the scruffy beard that hid the lower half of his face. Her silly heart danced a tango in her chest. Justin could crawl guerrilla-style into her house after spending a month battling through the wild forest that bordered Lake Itirangi, and Emily would still think he was the most striking man she'd ever laid eyes on. Hands down.

If childhood bullying was the first reason Emily hated Chloe Somers, then Justin Simons was the second.

"Justin," she said, her voice breathy. "What are you doing here?"

Did he know what today was?

Almost a year ago, Chloe had left him with the responsibility of cancelling their wedding while she skipped town with Rich. It couldn't be a coincidence that he was here now. Did he plan to sabotage the wedding? Try to win Chloe back? The town had been abuzz with speculation after Chloe ended their relationship so spectacularly, and Justin had retreated into his house by the forest, grown a beard, and barely spared a kind word for anyone since. His surliness didn't stop Emily's foolish heart from wishing he'd see her as something other than a little girl, or a friend of his sister.

"Scoping out the wedding," he replied gruffly, shifting from one foot to the other, as if he regretted saying hello and was itching to leave.

She shouldn't be offended. Justin seemed uncomfortable in *anyone's* presence these days. He was more of a loner, spending time with his family but few others. All of the locals desperately wanted to support him, but he wouldn't give them the chance.

"Why?" she asked, wondering if she'd been right about his plan to interfere.

He shrugged one massive shoulder. "I'm invited."

Like he'd pulled the pin on her emotional grenade, Emily exploded. "Oh, for fudge sake! Shiitake mushrooms on a stick with a side of flaming brownies. Are you kidding me right now?"

~

If anyone else had uttered the ridiculous expletives that had just passed between Emily Parker's pouty pink lips, Justin would have laughed in their face. But Emily looked so adorably angry on his behalf, her entire face flushed red and her tiny fists clenched, body shaking with rage, that he was oddly flattered. Everyone knew Emily was the nicest person in Itirangi, and for her to be furious like this? It meant something. She seemed ready to go to war for him. And Justin, dirty sonofabitch that he was, badly wanted to bend her over one of the dining tables and show her how much he appreciated her support.

Instead, he reigned in the impulse to defile Itirangi's favorite sweetheart and said, "I wouldn't joke about something like that."

"Please say you're not actually coming."

He wished he could. He'd rather be anywhere else. But Chloe and Rich had invited him to their super-romantic New Year's Eve wedding—even if they'd excluded the rest of his family, likely at Chloe's behest—and his pride wouldn't let him reject the invitation. He couldn't bear for them to assume he was pining for Chloe. He wasn't. He was well rid of her. End of story.

So here he was, getting the lay of the land, ready to venture into enemy territory come nightfall. Chloe and Rich had planned the wedding to culminate in a countdown to midnight, complete with fireworks at the moment the year changed. Very romantic, he was sure, for the bride and groom and anyone who had a date, but Justin didn't. He'd RSVP'd with a plus-one, but never got around to finding someone to accompany him. He needed someone trustworthy, but in Itirangi, very few people could be relied on not to gossip. Now that the day was here, he would happily go back in time and kick his own ass for not organizing some kind of moral support.

"I'm coming," he told her, deadly serious.

Emily folded her arms over her breasts, drawing his attention to the curves hidden by a high-necked shirt. He'd fantasized about running his hands over those curves dozens of times in the past few months. Ever since he'd recovered from Chloe's betrayal, Emily had become his obsession. Unfortunately, with her sweet nature and luscious body, Justin wasn't alone in desiring her. Every unattached male in Itirangi between the ages of fifteen and fifty adored her, and Emily was unfailingly friendly to all of them. Of course, she treated kicked puppies the same way. Justin hoped he was more to her than just another kicked puppy.

"But why?" she asked. "Why torture yourself like that? And why on earth would they invite you in the first place? It's too cruel."

He grunted in agreement. "That's what any normal person would think."

But not Chloe and Rich. He doubted it had occurred to them that inviting him would be anything other than polite. They weren't known for being particularly thoughtful people.

"Do you need a hand?" he asked.

That was why he'd come in, after all. He'd felt guilty hiding out in his car, watching Emily lug boxes of decorations back and forth, a job that would take half as much time if he helped.

"No, no, I'm fine." Her cheeks reddened again. "I don't have much left to do. I'm just putting everything together, adding the final touches."

"So tell me what to do and you can get out of here early." He wasn't backing off. Not when he finally had the opportunity for some alone time with Emily.

"Okay," she relented, and rummaged through one of the boxes for a roll of silver table runners he recognized from his own ill-fated wedding. Apparently, Chloe wasn't above recycling. "Put these down the center of the tables with the centerpieces on top. I'll sort out the candles."

Justin fumbled with the delicate fabric, doing his best to

lay the first one neatly, so she wouldn't regret accepting his help. He analyzed the runner. Was it off-center? He adjusted it to the right. Checked again. Better. Shifting to the next table, he repeated the actions.

Once he'd finished with the table runners, Emily slapped a pile of folded napkins into his hands and showed him how to distribute them, along with the menus, which were hand-written in a looping script he struggled to read. He could see signs of Chloe everywhere, and none of her fiancé. But then, perhaps Rich didn't mind someone else being in charge. Unlike Justin, who preferred to make decisions together.

He and Chloe had squabbled like children over just about everything when they were planning to get married: the venue, food, decorations, number of guests invited. Justin had wanted a casual wedding near the forest, while Chloe had wanted something high-end and less outdoorsy. His job as a park ranger had been a constant cause of friction between them. He'd mistakenly imagined they were one of those 'opposites attract' stories, but it turned out that wasn't what she'd wanted at all.

A light touch brushed his flannel-clad upper arm. "You okay?"

He came to with a jolt. Emily's unusual green eyes were watching him with concern. He focused on the darker band around her pupils.

"Fine," he snapped. He wasn't about to fall apart on her, and he'd appreciate it if she didn't look at him like he might. "What now?"

Emily's pulse hammered as she touched Justin. It was the first time she'd been brave enough to initiate contact, but he'd seemed so lost staring at the decorations, as if they held the answers to everything, that she couldn't help it.

She should have made him leave.

Bad enough he was attending the wedding, it must be awful to help her set it up when the memory of the decor he'd chosen for his wedding was still fresh.

"You go home," she said gently. "I shouldn't have taken advantage of your offer, but thank you for your help."

Justin scowled and brushed her off. "You're not sending me away that easy, Em."

"But—"

"No."

"Tell you what," she said, feeling uncharacteristically bold. "You tell me why you're going to the wedding and I'll let you stay and help me."

She didn't usually ask intrusive questions, but this was Justin, and she finally had him to herself. She'd ask what she wanted to and hopefully make an impression. And part of her really, really wanted to know if he pined after Chloe.

His eyes narrowed, and she thought he might tell her to go to hell, but then he spoke. "I need to save face. If I don't come, all of the old gossips will tear me apart."

"No, they won't!" Emily protested, horrified he'd believe that. Her hand flew to her chest. "Everyone around here loves you, Justin. They only want the best for you."

"But a little fodder for the gossip mill never hurt."

His shoulders were square, his expression stubborn. She could see she wouldn't win this battle, so she passed him a stack of chair covers and demonstrated how to put them in place.

"That easy," she said, tying the bow with a flourish.

Justin's first attempt was such a pitiful mess she couldn't help laughing. Initially indignant, he joined in when she snorted, her eyes widening in horror. She suspected he was laughing more at her snort than his poor efforts, but she went through the motions again, emphasizing each movement as he copied her.

"Like this. Slip it over, shimmy it down. Yes, yes, wait. Hang on a minute." She caught his hand, gnawing on her lower lip as she realized her mistake in touching him again. His callouses rubbed against her fingertips, sending a frisson of awareness up the inside of her arm. His quick intake of breath made her wonder if he'd felt electricity zap between them, too. She studied his hands discreetly, wondering whether the rest of him was equally well built.

Tearing her attention away, she corrected his mistake, and together they tidied up his second chair. He completed the third on his own, and it wasn't bad for a guy with such thick, rough fingers. They finished in under an hour. She cast an eye over his work, making sure it met her rigorous standards—she couldn't have an unhappy customer—then, before she lost her nerve, she hugged him.

Oh, my.

She'd known he was brawny, that much was obvious. Now, being pressed against a wall of muscle, she was inclined to think of him as the Incredible Hulk. All of that body mass made a girl feel delicate. She wanted to explore the bands of muscle with her hands, to learn the way they tensed when he was in the throes of passion.

But no, this was a simple thank you hug. At his ex's wedding venue for crying out loud. She shouldn't be lusting after him.

"Thank you," she said, lurching backward so quickly she narrowly avoided tripping over an empty box. "That would have taken me twice as long without you."

"We're done?"

"Sure are. I'll come back tomorrow to collect my things, but everything is finished for today."

He grunted. Did the man ever use his words?

"Are you certain about going tonight?" she asked, reluctant to let it go. "I can't talk you out of it?"

He nodded decisively. "I'm going. But..."

"But?"

He gazed into the distance for a moment and she wondered whether he'd ignored her, but then he leveled his intense hazel gaze on her. "It might make the time pass faster if you came with me."

Emily's head spun like she'd tripped head over heels into a different dimension. "Excuse me?"

"I understand if it would be too awkward for you," he said, his gaze slipping from hers. "Since you two never got along. But we had fun just now, didn't we?"

"We did," she replied slowly. "But Justin, it's the day of the wedding. You can't just add someone to the guest list."

"Not a problem," he declared. "I said I'd bring a date when I RSVP'd. But—"

"You were too embarrassed to ask anyone," she broke in, understanding immediately.

He shuffled from foot to foot, clearly nervous about her reply. His uncertainty was what undid her.

"Of course I'll come. I'd love to keep you company."

"Thanks." The word was short and sharp, but the gratitude in his eyes warmed her. He might not communicate well verbally, but his body language filled the gaps.

Her foolish heart flip-flopped. This was *Justin.* The prospect of seeing him in a suit had her panting in anticipation.

"I'll pick you up at six," he told her. "The ceremony starts at six thirty, then we'll have dinner. It ends at midnight. Does that suit?"

Emily nodded, worried if she spoke, she wouldn't be able to disguise her sudden eagerness for the evening ahead.

"Bye," she squeaked, as he left.

He lifted a hand in a casual wave.

ALSO BY ALEXA RIVERS

Little Sky Romance Novellas
Midnight Kisses

Second Chance Christmas

Little Sky Romances
Accidentally Yours

From Now Until Forever

It Was Always You

Dreaming of You

Haven Bay
Then There Was You

Two of a Kind

Safe in his Arms

If Only You Knew

Pretend to Be Yours

Begin Again With You

Let Me Love You

Destiny Falls
Stay With You

Come Back to You

Always Been Yours

ACKNOWLEDGMENTS

Since this is the last of the Little Sky Romances, I want to take the opportunity to thank everyone who has helped me while I've been writing the series. Thanks to my family for reading early drafts and offering advice, and to my beta readers—in particular to the ones who offered advice that wasn't necessarily easy to give (or take) but helped my stories immensely. A massive thank you to Kate S for being an awesome editor, and for all your contributions to my stories (and your enthusiasm). Thank you to Serena C for your thoughtful comments and for bringing consistency to my writing, and to Virginia, Carol and Lorna. Thank you to the judges of writing contests, who've provided constructive feedback along the way, to Deranged Doctor Design for my gorgeous covers, Lastly, thanks to everyone who has offered help, opinions, information and advice during my publishing journey. You're all wonderful.

ABOUT THE AUTHOR

Alexa Rivers writes about genuine characters living messy, imperfect lives and earning hard-won happily ever afters. Most of her books are set in small towns, and she lives in one of these herself. She shares a house with a neurotic dog and a husband who thinks he's hilarious.

When she's not writing, she enjoys traveling, baking, eating too much chocolate, cuddling fluffy animals, drinking excessive amounts of tea, and absorbing herself in fictional worlds.